THE DIARY OF NOBODY'S SON

THE DIARY OF NOBODY'S SON

Lupin Pooter

Psychology News Press

The Diary of Nobody's Son

Lupin Pooter

With contributions from his father Charles Pooter,
And some words and images by
George Grossmith & Weedon Grossmith

Psychology News Press

95–97 East Road London N1 6AW

Typeset by Keyboard Services, Luton, Beds.

Printed by Spauda in Lithuania.

ISBN 978-0-90-763358-7

Honour thy mother and thy father – that thy days may be long on the land that The Lord Thy God giveth thee, as it says in what pew folk call The Good Book.

I couldn't honour Pa with all my heart and soul, but I did love him which why I did not publish this book until after he and Ma passed away. I could afford to bury them in the cemetery in Highgate. Pa would have liked to rest with the best. The Highgate worms feast on what's left of Karl Marx, who became something of a hero for me, as well as of George Eliot, cousins of Charles Dickens and some of the Rossettis. The cemetery is also the last resting place for many of the very ghastly. Adam Worth, the 'Napoleon of crime', who may have inspired Conan Doyle to create Moriarty as a rival for Sherlock Holmes, rests there too.

Pa would have loved to keep such fine company when he popped his clogs. He'd have smacked me though if I ever suggested he popped clogs on in daily life. He liked to dress nicely and often didn't much like my get up.

I often baffled Pa and, sometimes, made him furious, but I knew he loved me, though he had as much clue about who I was as the cucumbers in my garden. I owe the phrase to Edmund Gosse, of whose cucumbers more later. He called his book *Father and Son*, "a study of two temperaments." There are surprisingly few books about fathers, sons and their conflicts. Where is a memoir that digs as deep as Hamlet? Every boy has a father so the subject is universal. Girls might even find it useful.

I didn't want to hurt Pa or my wonderful Ma, who would

have loved me whatever, and who I loved whatever. Loving whatever. That's what life should be about though it took me long enough to find out. So I bottled up my pen till they died.

Pa loved his puns. I can hear him say: "So, Lupin, you penned in your pen." I'd have laughed if I was in the mood to be the good son, which I sometimes was. And sometimes wasn't.

Still, I wish Pa hadn't called his book *The Diary of a Nobody*. There's a selfish reason; it makes me out to be nobody's son, in fact, nobody's only son, which makes me sound like I am less than nothing. But there's an unselfish

" The Laurels," Brickfield Terrace, Holloway.

Home Sweet Home

reason too. Pa had his moments when he was nothing like a nobody or, to be positive, something like a somebody.

This book is partly Pa's and partly mine as I comment on his diary – and especially on what it says about me. It's a dialogue between him and me, a dialogue we never had in real life because it would have been too difficult. To make it easy to follow the two voices, Pa's diary is in italics:

My dear wife Carrie and I have just been a week in our new house, "The Laurels," Brickfield Terrace, Holloway—a nice six-roomed residence, not counting basement, with a front breakfast-parlour. We have a little front garden; and there is a flight of ten steps up to the front door, which, by-the-by, we keep locked with the chain up. Cummings, Gowing, and our other intimate friends always come to the little side entrance, which saves the servant the trouble of going up to the front door, thereby taking her from her work. We have a nice little back garden which runs down to the railway. We were rather afraid of the noise of the trains at first, but the landlord said we should not notice them after a bit, and took £2 off the rent. He was certainly right; and beyond the cracking of the garden wall at the bottom, we have suffered no inconvenience.

Pa makes it clear he was well-off enough for him and Ma to have a servant, Sarah – of whom more later. He loved *The Laurels* because it was their first house. Before that they lived in rooms or, at the start of their marriage, in one room. He called Cummings and Gowing his intimate friends, and his diary has much to say about them, though we never find out much about their pasts. I thought this odd at the time, but all I will say for now is that: Cummings was not the man's real name.

Gowing did not work in the City as Pa assumed. The man or woman who writes a totally honest diary will deserve to be saint.

Pa saw the City as safe and respectable; he worshipped both adjectives. Every day he took the number 43 bus from Holloway to Monument, and then walked to his office in Houndsditch. He disliked the underground because his clothes would get dirty if he travelled on it and grimy clothes make you look as if you'd slept in a ditch.

Readers will, I hope, get used to a few digressions. Few people know the link between dry cleaning, which would eliminate Pa's grime problem, and racial equality. There is

Thomas "dry cleaning" Jennings – a man who created a new industry

one, however. On March 3, 1821, Thomas L. Jennings became the first African-American to get a United States patent, for his cleaning process called "dry scouring," which was the precursor to dry cleaning.

Thirty years later a French dye-worker, Jean Baptiste Jolly, stopped scouring and started nettoyage à sec—or dry cleaning. There were a few teething problems; Jolly used petroleum-based chemicals and trousers often caught fire while being cleaned. But dry cleaners kept on trying not to incinerate clothes, which was bad for business. During World War I, dry cleaners finally mastered the art of not combusting clothes.

Dry cleaners should have a coat of arms with the legend: 'Liar, liar, pants on fire.'

At heart, Pa was a homebody.

Pa when he painted the bath red by mistake

After my work in the City, I like to be at home. What's the good of a home, if you are never in it? "Home, Sweet Home," that's my motto.

You'd never guess that the man who praised Home Sweet Home was born far from respectable Holloway. You are where you started life in many ways. Because of where he was born, Pa often felt he wasn't good enough and that he'd be rumbled by his betters. In 1893, when he started to write his diary, he was, as he would say 'settled' as a middling clerk in a middling firm where he had worked for 21 years. Sometimes he makes it sound as if he had been born in one of the firm's ledgers.

Pa was as loyal as a barnacle to the firm and, most of all to his superior, Mr Perkupp. I've sometimes wondered whether Perkupp was his real name, or whether the old stick made it up, but Perkupp didn't have the imagination to imagine anything. At the time, a tonic called Perk U Uppo was all the rage. It claimed to put hairs on your chest, and to cure gout, sadness, badness, baldness, as well as the feeling I used to have when I was sixteen that there was no point in getting out of bed. Did Perkupp name himself after a tonic he smarmed himself in? It wouldn't surprise me. These days I don't languish in bed waiting for Ma to bring me a cup of tea and gently nag me to get up. I rise and shine with the sun. I whistle and wash with the birds. (Birds have excellent hygiene, I have learned. You never see a nightingale that hasn't done its ablutions.)

I don't need to perk up because I wake up as perked as a person can be.

I've decided to write this as I don't want the world to think I was the kind of man Pa often made me out to be.

In the diary, which started in April 1893, you'd never guess at first that he had a son. For its first four months, I don't exist and. then, I appear out of the blue as if Pa suddenly remembered me:

July 30.—The miserable cold weather is either upsetting me or Carrie, or both. We seem to break out into an argument about absolutely nothing, and this unpleasant state of things usually occurs at meal-times.

This morning, for some unaccountable reason, we were talking about balloons, and we were as merry as possible; but the conversation drifted into family matters, during which Carrie, without the slightest reason, referred in the most uncomplimentary manner to my poor father's pecuniary trouble. I retorted by saying that "Pa, at all events, was a gentleman," whereupon Carrie burst out crying. I positively could not eat any breakfast.

Pa's troubles were more than pecuniary, I would learn much later when I discovered some of his secrets.

Did I discover them all? I still wonder.

At the office I was sent for by Mr. Perkupp, who said he was very sorry, but I should have to take my annual holidays from next Saturday. Franching called at office and asked me to dine at his club, "The Constitutional." Fearing disagreeables at home after the "tiff" this morning, I sent a telegram to Carrie, telling her I was going out to dine and she was not to sit up. Bought a little silver bangle for Carrie.

July 31.—Carrie was very pleased with the bangle, which I left with an affectionate note on her dressing-table last night before going to bed. I told Carrie we should have to start for our holiday next Saturday. She replied quite happily that she did not mind, except that the weather was so bad, and she feared that Miss Jibbons would not be able to get her a seaside dress in time. I told Carrie that I thought the drab one with pink bows looked quite good enough; and Carrie said she should not think of wearing it. I was about to discuss the matter, when, remembering the argument yesterday, resolved to hold my tongue.

I said to Carrie: "I don't think we can do better than 'Good old Broadstairs.'" Carrie not only, to my astonishment, raised an objection to Broadstairs, for the first time; but begged me not to use the expression, "Good old," but to leave it to Mr. Stillbrook and other gentlemen of his type. Hearing my 'bus pass the window, I was obliged to rush out of the house without kissing Carrie as usual; and I shouted to her: "I leave it to you to decide." On returning in the evening, Carrie said she thought as the time was so short she had decided on Broadstairs, and had written to Mrs. Beck, Harbour View Terrace, for apartments.

He did usually kiss Ma. The nicest thing about him was that he adored her – and did not stint her dress allowance.

August 1.— Carrie has ordered of Miss Jibbons a pink Garibaldi and blue-serge skirt, which I always think looks so pretty at the seaside. In the evening she trimmed herself a little sailor-hat, while I read to her the Exchange and Mart. We had a good laugh over my trying on the hat when she had finished it; Carrie saying it looked so funny with my beard, and how the people would have roared if I went on the stage like it.

August 2.—Mrs. Beck wrote to say we could have our usual rooms at Broadstairs. That's off our mind. Bought a coloured shirt and a pair of tan-coloured boots, which I see many of the swell clerks wearing in the City, and hear are all the "go."

August 3.—A beautiful day. Looking forward to tomorrow. Carrie bought a parasol about five feet long. I told her it was ridiculous. She said: "Mrs. James, of Sutton, has one twice as long so;" the matter dropped. I bought a capital hat for hot weather at the seaside. I don't know what it is called, but it is the shape of the helmet worn in India, only made of straw. Got three new ties, two coloured handkerchiefs, and a pair of navy-blue socks at Pope Brothers. Spent the evening packing. Carrie told me not to forget to borrow Mr. Higgsworth's telescope, which he always lends me, knowing I know how to take care of it. Sent Sarah out for it. While everything was seeming so bright, the last post brought us a letter from Mrs. Beck, saying: "I have just let all my house to one party, and am sorry I must take back my words, and am sorry you must find other apartments; but Mrs. Womming, next door, will be pleased to accommodate you, but she cannot take you before Monday, as her rooms are engaged Bank Holiday week."

It is at this moment of crisis that I get my first mention.

August 4.—The first post brought a nice letter from our dear son Willie, acknowledging a trifling present which Carrie sent him, the day before yesterday being his twentieth birthday.

To our utter amazement he turned up himself in the

afternoon, having journeyed all the way from Oldham. He said he had got leave from the bank, and as Monday was a holiday he thought he would give us a little surprise.

August 5, Sunday.—We have not seen Willie since last Christmas, and are pleased to notice what a fine young man he has grown. One would scarcely believe he was Carrie's son. He looks more like a younger brother. I rather disapprove of his wearing a check suit on a Sunday, and I think he ought to have gone to church this morning; but he said he was tired after yesterday's journey, so I refrained from any remark on the subject. We had a bottle of port for dinner, and drank dear Willie's health.

You may begin to understand why I feel I have to write this book before I join the good and grave in Highgate. I only have to appear in the diary for Pa to "rather disapprove" of me. He doesn't like the fact that I don't go to church, because not going

Pa did not catch me looking at my best in his diary

marked you out. If there were any atheists in Holloway in 1893, they kept their radical opinions to themselves. Then he thought my suit unsuitable. Was that fair?

Did I go to church in my underpants? Or naked? Or wearing a loincloth?

No, I went in a check suit. The real problem was that I was noticeable. Pa didn't want to be noticed too much, or noticed for the wrong thing. His ambition was that I should be like him. Safe, steady and a respectable nobody.

But even nobodies have some history. You'd hardly guess from the diary, however. Pa did not reveal that after he and mother married they could not live either with my father's family or my mother's. So they had to rent a room you couldn't swing the proverbial cat in. It was there, on one of the less salubrious streets around Old Street, I came into the world.

I was born in 1875. My first memory was of that small room in which we slept, ate and Ma worked mending clothes for a few much needed pennies. There was an inside privy on the landing which we shared with three families whose hygiene would have appalled any well-bred nightingale. Is it a coincidence that the great nurse, who was mustard keen on hygiene, was called Nightingale?

Despite the germs, I survived to be christened at St Luke's on Old Street though I have absolutely no memory of being dunked in the font.

I knew Pa would be annoyed soon after I got home. His diary records the first of many arguments we were to have over the next year, the year in which after trials and tribulations, I became a man. Pa wrote:

"Oh, by-the-by, did I tell you I've cut my first name, 'William,' and taken the second name 'Lupin'? In fact, I'm only known at Oldham as 'Lupin Pooter.' If you were to 'Willie' me there, they wouldn't know what you meant."

The idea that I was not Willie in Oldham made Pa sigh – and he sighed even more when he realised Ma did not agree with him:

Of course, Lupin being a purely family name, Carrie was delighted, and began by giving a long history of the Lupins. I ventured to say that I thought William a nice simple name, and reminded him he was christened after his Uncle William, who was much respected in the City.

You may well wonder why I was not named after my either my mother's father, or my father's father, but after Uncle William, who was himself no king of nobs or snobs. Pa made it sound as if I were being rude when I piped up as he wrote:

Willie, in a manner which I did not much care for, said sneeringly: "Oh, I know all about that—Good old Bill!" and helped himself to a third glass of port.

"Good old Bill" was not, in fact, well-known in the City, which is why Pa did not give the kind of details one might expect - such as that Good old Bill was a Stockbroker in the ancient and glorious firm of Moneybags or Senior Clerk in the well-respected house of Shekel and Sons.

Many diaries include a family tree but Pa's diary did not

include any such arboreal. He does not elaborate on "the long history of the Lupins". At first I was surprised, but the more I found out about the history of the Lupins, the less surprised I was. We are all curious about our ancestors. It took me some effort, and a little money, to piece together my family history.

My grandmother had been an under-maid at Elspeth Manor which belonged to the Philpott family who had made their fortune in chutneys. She was a pretty girl and pretty maids often attract the attentions, wanted and unwanted, of the sons of the house. There were three boys in the family. Charles was nineteen and had already decided to be a clergyman; Daniel was destined for the Navy and Zephirah was bound for Cambridge, but he did not do well there and eventually went into the family business. He turned out to have a gift for devising new chutneys. Zephirah was also very religious and believed, that when Christ fed the five thousand, he provided them not just with loaves and fishes, but with chutneys too. Inexplicably the Gospels left out that detail, perhaps because it was too spicy. Zephirah also had the idea of advertising his chutneys by paying for a book to be written about them.

Irene, my grandmother, would never say which of the three Philpotts was the father. She may not have known. She was an under maid and 'under' was the right word. It could have been any of them as each of them persuaded her to tumble in the grass under them. It was hardly unusual in 1850s for the young bucks of rich families to poddle the servants. (The word poddle no longer seems to be uscd in this sense, but its meaning is clear). It was also common to send 'fallen' girls – well, they had fallen on their backs – to the local asylum or the poor house. Irene must have had something though. Each of the boys insisted that he had not seduced her so that it had to be one of the village boys, but they also insisted their parents make arrangements to board the child, my future mother, out. The boys said that was the Christian way.

So Ma was brought up for many years by Margaret, who had been one of the servants at Elspeth Manor until her eyesight began to fail and she could no longer see the dirt in the corners she had to sweep. Then the family put her in a small cottage on their estate and allowed her a meagre pension, which they did increase when she had my mother to care for.

To put my grandmother in an asylum would not have been very Christian, but to let her return to the house would have been too Christian. So she was found a job with a different family who gloried in an army of servants and under-servants. She had a gift for making pies and devoted herself for nearly half a century to baking steak and oyster, steak and kidney and a pie which sounds exotic, cod and curry, my mother told me eventually. If Irene, who was now an under-cook, continued her 'undering' I don't know.

The three sons, Irene's lovers, made sure my mother got the appropriate education for her class. So she went to primary school – and learned her letters.

"I never told your father who my true mother was," Ma told me after he had died. "I said she had died in hospital."

Sometimes Ma visited her mother secretly, telling Pa she had been asked to deliver laundry to people in another part

Queen Victoria was not amused by such goings-on

of London. She left early in the morning and was always back by six.

I did not know then that Pa had an even more shameful secret.

When he was old and sick, I pressed him to tell me about his youth. After much pleading, Pa he finally told me he had been born in Whitechapel. His mother abandoned him so he was brought up in a poor house. His first job was at a grocer's where he helped add up what the customers owed. He was given board, lodging and five shillings a week. He often had to deliver goods and, sometimes, he would be given a small tip. He spent these tips on smokes– and on visiting dancing halls. He wanted to dance well not just to impress girls but also, I came to suspect, because if you could waltz, you were a cut above the lowest working class.

In his diary Pa mentions dancing – and an invitation he never expected.

April 30.—Perfectly astounded at receiving an invitation for Carrie and myself from the Lord and Lady Mayoress to the Mansion House, to "meet the Representatives of Trades and Commerce." My heart beat like that of a schoolboy's. Carrie and I read the invitation over two or three times. I could scarcely eat my breakfast. I said—and I felt it from the bottom of my heart,—"Carrie darling, I was a proud man when I led you down the aisle of the church on our wedding-day; that pride will be equalled, if not surpassed, when I lead my dear, pretty wife up to the Lord and Lady Mayoress at the Mansion House." I saw the tears in Carrie's eyes, and she said: "Charlie dear, it is I who have to be proud of you. And I am very, very proud of you. You have called me pretty; and as long as I am pretty in your eyes, I am happy. You, dear old Charlie, are not handsome, but you are good, which is far more noble." I gave her a kiss, and she said: "I wonder if there will be any dancing? I have not danced with you for years."

I cannot tell what induced me to do it, but I seized her round the waist, and we were silly enough to be executing a wild kind of polka when Sarah entered, grinning, and said: "There is a man, mum, at the door who wants to know if you want any good coals." Most annoyed at this.

I can hardly blame Pa because he wanted to enjoy the fact that he had been invited to consort with high society. As soon as he had finished with the coal man, he got back to the intricacies of answering the invitation to Mansion House. A confident man would have rattled back a simple 'delighted to attend', but he wanted to get it perfect as if he worried they might send a telegram saying the invitation had been a mistake.

Spent the evening in answering, and tearing up again, the reply to the Mansion House, having left word with Sarah if Gowing or Cummings called we were not at home. Must consult Mr. Perkupp how to answer the Lord Mayor's invitation.

Perkupp would have the answer about the answer. I suspect Pa thought his flawless superior was a regular at all the best tables and that the Queen herself had consulted him on her investments. I sometimes dream that he dreamed of waltzing with Mr Perkupp.

But if Pa had not liked dancing, I'd never have been.

My parents met at Caldwell's 'dancing-rooms' at 32 Dean Street at the corner of Bateman Street. When I went there some 25 years later, it was one of the seediest, shabbiest tumble-down dance spots you could find even in Soho. It cost 1/6 to get in. There were some old handbills on the walls. In 1872, when my parents met there it cost eight pence to dance, which was not cheap when £1 a week was a decent wage.

At the entrance of the rundown place sat a rundown man, who had a glass of rum and water before him. Rumdown (for he downed the rum) told me the place had not changed for years. Up the staircase, there was a mirror spotted with brown and the two cracked, plaster statues in the dancing-room also had brown flecks. The dancing room was a large bare space whose decoration was very tatty.

One end of it was a gallery where the "music" sat. The band was seedy with its cornet cracked and the men who played the other instruments not up to much. Caldwell's was full of girls called "dolly-mops", slang for semi prostitutes. Ballet girls out of an engagement and "slaveys" out for the night also patronised it; and the men who went there were almost all snobs or cads who just wanted the obvious.

When Ma had first got to London, not knowing what the place was like, she and two friends went to Caldwells – and a young man asked her if she would dance.

"Why not," she said.

Pa often said was that the moment he led her out on to the dance floor, she fell in love with him. Ma would smile at that. Enigmatically.

At the end of the evening, he asked to walk her home. "I'll go by myself," she said tartly.

The truth was she did not want him to see she was living in a fine house in Hammersmith, but that she had to go in by the servants' stairs in the basement. She was an under-maid like her mother had been.

"When can I see you next," he asked outside the dance hall.

She agreed to see him on Saturday night.

"Why not before?"

"Girls have their secrets," Ma said.

Her secret, of course, was that she only had one night off a week. Every other night she waited downstairs, washing dishes, mopping floors, polishing the silver till the bell summoned her to bring tea or brandy to her masters.

After two months of walking out together, they decided to connube. Like poddle, it's a word that is not much used these days. To connube was to live together as if in connubial bliss, but without the actual marriage having taken place. We think of the 1870s as very respectable but London was a city of many morals. The upper and middle classes were bound by conventions. You had to be married if you were to couple, but the lower orders often didn't bother. A wedding cost more than they could afford. George Bernard Shaw got it right in *Pygmalion* where Alfred Doolittle, the eloquent dustman, lives happily in sin with Elisa's mother till he gets rich – and then he has to appear in church in top hat and tails, and tie the knot of respectability.

My parents did not tie the knot until Ma became pregnant. She then insisted on a wedding because she felt it would be sinful to have a bastard child. They weren't married in church but in the registry office at St Pancras.

I will not say more of my arrival into the world as I don't remember it at all but it must have happened. I'll skip ahead to what happened on August 5th and 6th 1893 when I got back from Oldham. It was after I had mentioned "Good old Bill", that Pa said something which I had been dreading. He said:

"My dear Willie, I hope you are happy with your colleagues at the Bank."

There wasn't much I could say without lying. I was employed at Martins Bank in Oldham, a grimy city and one of the founding clubs of the Football League. Martins Bank had just opened a branch there. The bank had been started in 1553 and was famous for its Grasshopper, the sign under which the bank traded. I made it my business to learn a little of the bank. The Martin family were among the early London Goldsmiths. In 1558, Richard Martin was a Lord Mayor of the City of London. Or as Karl Marx might put it – the Most Capital of the Capitalists.

The bank should have ditched the sign after La Fontaine's *Fables* became a classic. In one fable, *La Cigale et La Fourmi*, or the Grasshopper and the Ant, the grasshopper skips about in pursuit of perpetual pleasure while the diligent ant builds up provisions – or capital for the future. The hedonist and the safe and steady. Come bleak mid-winter, the grasshopper starves while the ant has plenty of grub.

Like most banks then, Martins was old fashioned. After the collapse of Barings Bank in 1890, however, Martins

turned itself into a limited company, that splendid capitalist device which meant the partners wouldn't be liable for the debts if it went bust. They opened branches in the north, around Manchester and Liverpool. And Oldham.

"This is an old and honourable bank, Pooter," said the balding man with a round face who was in charge of us clerks.

"Yes, Mr Down," I replied.

Down was a good name for him as he was always putting us clerks down.

"We expect employees to arrive on time," he smiled because he thought he was going to say something devilish clever," time and time again."

"Yes, Mr Down," I said putting on my humble face.

If you were a junior clerk, you had to practice being humble from the moment you got in till you left at the end of the day.

"But time and time again you are not on time," Mr Down said. "I might be able to forgive that sometimes but other aspects of your conduct are not what we expect. We do not expect junior employees, especially those who have been with us just a few weeks, to make suggestions."

"Yes, Mr Down, but may I suggest..."

"I wonder if you are capable of not making suggestions which are of no interest to me at all."

He waved me to my desk. My suggestion had been utterly sensible. The best I thought was that we should leave a book in the foyer of the bank, so customers could make comments and offer ideas on how we might improve our service.

I don't think Pa ever exchanged a cross word with Mr Perkupp, or dared suggest a suggestion unless it was suggested he suggest one. So I thought it best not to tell Pa what I did next.

After work had finished on this no suggestion day, I walked through Oldham and found the nearest varieties shop. Oldham had one professional theatre, a number of music halls and a number of venues where amateurs performed. I soon found what I wanted.

The next day I appeared at the bank in my best suit – and something which was guaranteed to provoke comment.

"What do you think you are wearing," Mr Down spluttered when he saw me.

"As you can see, Mr Down, a dog muzzle. I bought it at the pantomime shop. To muzzle myself and so ensure I will not make any more unwelcome suggestions."

"You young hound," Mr Down shouted.

Two of the other clerks giggled at his unintended pun, which did not please him.

"You young scoundrel," he corrected himself. "How long have you worked here?"

"Three months."

"Three months too many. You will not work here one moment more. Take your belongings and go now."

I intend to be fairly honest, which is why I include the following. As I gathered my only belonging, my pen, I also removed a few sheets of paper headed Martins Bank, Oldham. I suspected that I would be glad of this as it would allow me to write an account of my last days at the bank, an account I suspected Pa would at some point insist on seeing.

It is, of course, lamentable for a son to resort to such tricks, but I knew Pa would be angry, and when he got angry, he was quite capable of slapping me. You would never guess that from the way he describes his behaviour. I do not say he slapped me often but I do recall a number of incidents. That is all I will say.

It was not really Pa's fault as I will explain. Fathers and sons love and hate each other, one of the key findings of the new-fangled psychology which became popular during the Great War. To make the point I will quote *Father and Son* by Edmund Gosse. Gosse lost his mother when he was eight which meant that he and his father became very close. He said:

"Sometimes in the course of this winter, my Father and I had long cosy talks together over the fire. Our favourite subject was murders. I wonder whether little boys of eight, soon to go upstairs alone at night, often discuss violent crime with a widower-papa. The practice, I cannot help thinking, is unusual; it was, however, consecutive with us. We tried other secular subjects, but we were sure to come around at last to 'what do you suppose they really did with the body?' I was told, a thrilled listener, the adventure of Mrs. Manning, who killed a gentleman on the stairs and buried him in quick-lime in the back-kitchen, and it was at this time that I learned the useful historical fact, which abides with me after half a century, that Mrs. Manning was hanged in black satin, which thereupon went wholly out of fashion in England. I also heard about Burke and Hare, whose story nearly froze me into stone with horror.

These were crimes which appear in the chronicles. But who will tell me what 'the Carpet-bag Mystery' was, which my Father and I discussed evening after evening? I have never come across a whisper of it since, and I suspect it of having been a hoax. As I recall the details, people in a boat, passing down the Thames, saw a carpet-bag hung high in air, on one of the projections of a pier of Waterloo Bridge. Being with difficulty dragged down—or perhaps up—this bag was found to be full of human remains, dreadful butcher's business of joints and fragments. Persons were missed, were identified, were again denied—the whole is a vapour in my memory which shifts as I try to define it. But clear enough is the picture I hold of myself, in a high chair, on the left-hand side of the sitting-room fireplace, the leaping flames reflected in the glass-case of tropical insects on the opposite wall, and my Father, leaning anxiously forward, with uplifted finger, emphasizing to me the pros and cons of the horrible carpet-bag evidence.

I suppose that my interest in these discussions—and Heaven knows I was animated enough—amused and distracted my Father, whose idea of a suitable theme for childhood's ear now seems to me surprising. I soon found that these subjects were not welcome to everybody, for, starting the Carpet-bag Mystery one morning with Miss Marks, in the hope of delaying my arithmetic lesson, she fairly threw her apron over her ears, and told me, from that vantage, that if I did not desist at once, she should scream."

It was all love between father and son when young Gosse was eight but it did not stay so sweet as the boy grew into his temperament. By the time Gosse was eighteen, he was at odds with his father. So I was not so odd in having problems with my Pa.

And my Pa was upset by his Pa who was not involved in the Carpet bag mystery, but knew a number of men who had been convicted of crimes.

"How," you ask.

He shared digs with them. Digs he could not dig his way out of.

"How," you ask again.

The digs were a cell. There were bars but not the kind where you have a snifter. Grandpa had been convicted of robbery with violence when he attacked a bank. I wish it had been Martins but, in 1855, Martins only had premises in London. With less brain than Martins' grasshopper, Grandpa burst into the First Bank of Northampton, threatened everyone with a gun and stole the massive sum of £50. He forgot to wear a mask and so he was recognised. He was caught later that day and sentenced to ten years in prison,

INTERIOR OF CELL.

An idea of Grandpa's digs

which he served in a grim place called The Verne. After he came out, he took to drink and soon died. He was buried in a pauper's grave.

This was something my father never spoke of – and something I only discovered much later. Pa did not even know where his father was buried. Inevitably Pa spoke little of his father. Before the robbery, Grandpa had made one of the local girls pregnant. Pa told us that his mother had died of typhoid, but I suspect she just abandoned him at the door of the poor house.

My ancestors really had done their children few favours. But their histories explain Pa's desperate need to be respectable. And for his only son to be respectable. Respectable also meant getting up early, even on holidays.

August 6, Bank Holiday.—As there was no sign of Lupin moving at nine o'clock, I knocked at his door, and said we usually breakfasted at half-past eight, and asked how long would he be? Lupin replied that he had had a lively time of it, first with the train shaking the house all night, and then with the sun streaming in through the window in his eyes, and giving him a cracking headache. Carrie came up and asked if he would like some breakfast sent up, and he said he could do with a cup of tea, and didn't want anything to eat.

Lupin not having come down, I went up again at half-past one, and said we dined at two; he said he "would be there." He never came down till a quarter to three. I said: "We have not seen much of you, and you will have to return by the 5.30 train; therefore you will have to leave in an hour, unless you go by the midnight mail." He said: "Look here, Guv'nor, it's no use beating about the bush. I've tendered my resignation at the Bank."

For a moment I could not speak. When my speech came again, I said: "How dare you, sir? How dare you take such a serious step without consulting me? Don't answer me, sir!—you will sit down immediately, and write a note at my dictation, withdrawing your resignation and amply apologising for your thoughtlessness."

Imagine my dismay when he replied with a loud guffaw: "It's no use. If you want the good old truth, I've got the chuck!"

I did not explain the full extent of the dog muzzle drama, of course. Pa would never have seen the joke. Instead, with a great show of reluctance, I finally showed him the letter which it seemed Mr Down at the bank had written. If you are a clerk you learn to write in many ways.

The letter which, of course, I had written, said:

Mr Pooter has unfortunately not arrived at work on time even though I have often allowed him considerable leeway. He took no interest in his work, and always arrived an hour (sometimes two hours) late. He is quite a capable young man but in the circumstances I felt it impossible to continue his employment.

Pa was angry, distraught, worried about the disgrace, worried about me – and worried about the holiday he and Ma had planned. He got a week's holiday a year and was determined it should be memorable.

August 7.—Mr. Perkupp has given me leave to postpone my holiday a week, as we could not get the room. This will give us an opportunity of trying to find an appointment for Willie before we go. The ambition of my life would be to get him into Mr. Perkupp's firm.

August 11.—Although it is a serious matter having our boy Lupin on our hands, still it is satisfactory to know he was asked to resign from the Bank simply because "he took no interest in his work, and always arrived an hour (sometimes two hours) late."

Pa had edited the letter for his diary and then got stuck into his description of the holiday. Having nothing better to do, I tagged along. Pa said:

We can all start off on Monday to Broadstairs with a light heart. This will take my mind off the worry of the last few days.

August 13.—Hurrah! at Broadstairs. Very nice apartments near the station. On the cliffs they would have been double the price. The landlady had a nice five o'clock dinner and tea ready, which we all enjoyed, though Lupin seemed fastidious because there happened to be a fly in the butter. It was very wet in the evening, for which I was thankful, as it was a good excuse for going to bed early. Lupin said he would sit up and read a bit.

Is it fastidious to complain because a fly has landed in the butter? As I recall Pa got it wrong – the fly was in the oxtail soup actually. Diaries are never totally truthful, but why lie about the location of the fly? I don't say Pa was fibbing; he may just have got a fly in his ointment to add, as he often did, a bad pun. As I write this, I wonder if Pa really did write his diary every night as he claimed. I suspect Pa mentioned the fly because it was a prelude to something he found difficult to write about, something I had done, as it was not the kind of thing a respectable young man was supposed to do:

August 14.—I was a little annoyed to find Lupin, instead of reading last night, had gone to a common sort of entertainment, given at the Assembly Rooms. I expressed my opinion that such performances were unworthy of respectable patronage; but he replied: "Oh, it was only 'for one night only.' I had a fit of the blues come on, and thought I would go to see Polly Presswell, England's Particular Spark." I told him I was proud to say I had never heard of her.

Carrie said: "Do let the boy alone. He's quite old enough to take care of himself, and won't forget he's a gentleman. Remember, you were young once yourself."

Pa snorted at the idea. He was born respectable he wanted us to think. Pa did love Ma and so he did not quarrel with her. He merely said that mothers are always on the side of their sons. He went on to complain that, though it was raining, I insisted on going out. I was afraid that if I were cooped up with them, Pa and I would quarrel again. And so was Pa it seems.

August 15.—Cleared up a bit, so we all took the train to Margate, and the first person we met on the jetty was Gowing. I said: "Hulloh! I thought you had gone to Barmouth with your Birmingham friends?" He said: "Yes, but young Peter Lawrence was so ill, they postponed their visit, so I came down here. You know the Cummings' are here too?" Carrie said: "Oh, that will be delightful! We must have some evenings together and have games."

I introduced Lupin, saying: "You will be pleased to find we have our dear boy at home!" Gowing said: "How's that? You don't mean to say he's left the Bank?"

I opened my mouth to explain some of the circumstances – I was sure Gowing would find the dog muzzle tale amusing – when Pa put a stop to that.

I changed the subject quickly, and thereby avoided any of those awkward questions which Gowing always has a knack of asking.

Avoiding awkward questions was one of Pa's hobbies. I was miffed he had muzzled me so tit for tat, I got my own back.

Pa in his silly helmet

August 16.—Lupin positively refused to walk down the Parade with me because I was wearing my new straw helmet with my frock-coat. I don't know what the boy is coming to.

The boy who had made the mistake of wearing a check suit had no intention of being seen with his father looking like a scarecrow who hoped to be invited to a formal dinner. In case readers can't imagine Pa in this rig out, the picture above shows all.

By the next day, we needed time away from each other, as Pa realised:

August 17.—Lupin not falling in with our views, Carrie and I went for a sail. It was a relief to be with her alone; for when Lupin irritates me, she always sides with him. On our return, he said: "Oh, you've been on the 'Shilling Emetic,' have you?

Pa's diary sometimes makes me out to be always drinking

You'll come to six-pennorth on the 'Liver Jerker' next." I presume he meant a tricycle, but I affected not to understand him.

Pa did not know that I had talked to Ma. When I got her on her own, I told her some of the truth about leaving the bank.

"That showed no respect for your superior," she said.

I hoped she would laugh, but all I got was a tiny smile at the dog muzzle tale.

"You know your father worries," she said.

"I saved some money," I reassured her, "so I won't need to borrow any."

"What a clever boy you are."

It was true that I had some money but that had nothing to do with saving.

A month before I got the chuck, I went to the racecourse at Haydock Park and placed a bet of ten shillings on an outsider, Martha's Vineyard. I liked the name. Martha liked the course and she romped in at 25-1. So I got £13 as you got your stake back too.

I was tempted to place more bets but as I worried – worrying inevitably was in my make up too – that I was not pleasing the bank and might need some savings, so I pocketed the winnings.

I was Boy Prudence … well not quite. There are many things that it's best for the most loving mother not to know, though. When I went to Oldham I had hardly even walked out with a girl.

The town had many music halls and public houses. There were the very cheap ones and ones which cost a little more. I sometimes went and downed a pint or two while I enjoyed the rattle-skattle acts. But the point of these halls wasn't just the entertainment on the stage. Off stage had its attractions. In the pubs by the theatre, there were girls, respectable girls – and girls who if they had ever been respectable had long stopped being that. There was no way I could afford to buy one of them a drink until Martha's Vineyard romped in at 25-1. The wildest pub was the Ma Egerton. Being careful of my £13 as the place was full of pickpockets, I bought a pint of best and sat down. A pretty redhead smiled at me.

"Where's your girl," she laughed.

"Not here," I laughed.

"Do you have a girl?"

"What's that to you?"

"I don't nick boys. Don't want to waste my breath on someone else's goods," she said. "I'm called Rosie."

I bought Rosie a pint, then another pint. We settled ourselves in a cosy corner.

"Where did you get the lolly?"

"I won on the horses."

"How much?"

"How much for what," I said.

Rosie put her hand on my thigh. "You ever done it before?"

"Lots of times," I said.

"Liar," she grinned. "Give me two pounds and we'll go to my room."

"Two pounds?"

"You'll get your money's worth," she smiled.

Rosie wasn't older than me in years, but she was years ahead of me in life.

We sauntered out of the pub and down past the bank. It sprung the devil in me. I put my arms around her and tried to kiss her.

"Not so fast," she smiled. She didn't kiss me but held me and slipped her hands in my pocket and – clearly it was something she was used to doing – and found half a crown.

"It's worth this," she said as she kissed me. "Like this," she said. "You open your mouth and lick my tongue with your tongue." She smiled: "I won't diddle you. Well," she laughed, "I will but you'll like it."

When we got to her house, she said we had to be quiet. We tiptoed up the stairs.

Her room had two chairs, a table and a bed. Her clothes hung in the wardrobe. She took off her jacket and hung it up neatly. She was wearing a white blouse. Through it, I could see her breasts.

"I bet you haven't done this," she laughed. Then she took my hands and put them on her breasts. "Have you ever seen such a fine pair of pears?"

She took off her blouse. She was right. I had never seen, never touched, never kissed. Rosie was, I discovered, a natural red-head.

It was two pounds well spent.

"Can I see you again," I asked as we lay naked on her bed.

"As long as you've got my wages," she grinned. "The wages of sin. Now you better hop it."

She gave me another kiss which was meant to end our larking. But I was ready to start again.

"You want seconds," she laughed. "Greedy."

But she let me have seconds.

"Now really hop it," she said as I gave her the two pounds.

I went back two days later when I said I only had a £1 left.

Rosie was a good sort. "It'll do," she said.

After Rosie had her wages of sin, I had nine pounds left. I spent five shillings buying a packet of decent cigars, not the tupenny ones which flake to bits as you puff. I bought them as I thought they'd impress Pa and his two intimate friends.

To return to Broadstairs, I wondered why Gowing and Cummings had followed us and how they had managed to arrange to have their holidays at exactly the same time. Gowing, I discovered years later, had a share in a draper's shop and had nothing whatever to do with the City. So he could take holidays whenever he wanted, but he thought having half a shop would never impress anyone so he pretended to work in the City.

The truth about Cummings I only discovered much later.

August 18.—Gowing and Cummings walked over to arrange an evening at Margate. It being wet, Gowing asked Cummings to accompany him to the hotel and have a game of billiards, knowing I never play, and in fact disapprove of the game. Cummings said he must hasten back to Margate; whereupon Lupin, to my horror, said: "I'll give you a game, Gowing—a hundred up. A walk round the cloth will give me an appetite for dinner." I said: "Perhaps Mister Gowing does not care to play with boys." Gowing surprised me by saying: "Oh yes, I do, if they play well," and they walked off together.

Gowing was a decent player. We each won one frame and he wanted to bet two bob on the decider. I won. When I told

Pa, he was amazed Gowing was quite good. (When I knew the truth about Gowing I realised he spent much time practicing billiards, as he only worked in his half shop half the time.)

"I've got gifts you don't know Pa," I said.

"Don't cheek your Pa," Ma said nicely.

It was sometimes not easy to be the obliging son Pa wanted, as one of his other hobbies was telling me what to do. Or usually what not to do.

August 19, Sunday.—I was about to read Lupin a sermon on smoking (which he indulges in violently) and billiards, but he put on his hat and walked out. Carrie then read me a long sermon on the palpable inadvisability of treating Lupin as if he were a mere child. I felt she was somewhat right, so in the evening I offered him a cigar. He seemed pleased, but, after a few whiffs, said: "This is a good old tup'ny—try one of mine," and he handed me a cigar as long as it was strong, which is saying a good deal.

August 20.—I am glad our last day at the seaside was fine, though clouded overhead. We went over to Cummings' (at Margate) in the evening, and as it was cold, we stayed in and played games; Gowing, as usual, overstepping the mark.

Gowing then said: "Are you a believer in the Great Mogul?" We had to answer all together: "Yes—oh, yes!" (three times). Gowing said: "So am I," and suddenly got up. The result of this stupid joke was that we all fell on the ground, and poor Carrie banged her head against the corner of the fender. Mrs. Cummings put some vinegar on; but through this we missed the last train, and had to drive back to Broadstairs, which cost me seven-and-sixpence.

Money, money, money. Pa was always worrying about it, and my future. Looking back I'm surprised he didn't come out in anxiety spots. His dream was to find me a job, where if I was steady and made no suggestions, I might at the age of fifty be making two pounds a week. To be fair, he did send many letters out in search of that 'berth' he wanted for me. He had even written from Broadstairs.

August 22.—Home sweet Home again! Carrie bought some pretty blue-wool mats to stand vases on. Fripps, Janus and Co. write to say they are sorry they have no vacancy among their staff of clerks for Lupin.

August 23.—I bought a pair of stags' heads made of plaster-of-Paris and coloured brown. They will look just the thing for our little hall, and give it style; the heads are excellent imitations. Poolers and Smith are sorry they have nothing to offer Lupin.

August 24.—Simply to please Lupin, and make things cheerful for him, as he is a little down, Carrie invited Mrs. James to come up from Sutton and spend two or three days with us. We have not said a word to Lupin, but mean to keep it as a surprise.

Mrs James wasn't a pleasant surprise. She was a pest who believed in the occult. Mr James had gone to the other side – anything to get away from her I thought – and was constantly telling her that he missed her by rapping on tables in Morse code. I wondered how Mr James knew Morse code as, while he was alive, he worked as a tea merchant and I'd never heard tea merchants used Morse. When I asked Mrs James how her 'dear departed' had learned Morse, she said we had no idea what you could learn on the other side, giving the impression that there were heavenly courses available in higher mathematics, French and embroidery. Even the parents you hold dear have their oddities and one of Ma's was that she didn't just like Mrs James, but thought her wise. I thought Mrs James was an old trout. Four days after she had arrived, Pa had bad news again.

August 27.—Carrie and Mrs. James went off shopping, and had not returned when I came back from the office. Judging from the subsequent conversation, I am afraid Mrs. James is filling Carrie's head with a lot of nonsense about dress. I walked over to Gowing's and asked him to drop in to supper, and make things pleasant.

Carrie prepared a little extemporised supper, consisting of the remainder of the cold joint, a small piece of salmon (which I was to refuse, in case there was not enough to go round), and a blanc-mange and custards. There was also a decanter of port and some jam puffs on the sideboard. Mrs. James made us play rather a good game of cards, called "Muggings." To my surprise, in fact disgust, Lupin got up in the middle, and, in a most sarcastic tone, said: "Pardon me, this sort of thing is too fast for me, I shall go and enjoy a quiet game of marbles in the back-garden."

Things might have become rather disagreeable but for Gowing (who seems to have taken to Lupin) suggesting they should invent games. Lupin said: "Let's play 'monkeys.'" He then led Gowing all round the room, and brought him in front of the looking-glass. I must confess I laughed heartily at this. I was a little vexed at everybody subsequently laughing at some joke which they did not explain, and it was only on going to bed I discovered I must have been walking about all the evening with an antimacassar on one button of my coat-tails.

August 28.—Found a large brick in the middle bed of geraniums, evidently come from next door. Pattles and Pattles can't find a place for Lupin.

Pa told me that when we were alone.

"Thank you for trying," I said.

"We have to find you a berth," he replied.

"I'm not a boat," I pointed out.

"You're rudderless. Or up the creek without a paddle."

I laughed which did not please Pa, who was already showing signs of nerves because Ma seemed so taken with Mrs James.

August 29.—Mrs. James is making a positive fool of Carrie. Carrie appeared in a new dress like a smock-frock. She said "smocking" was all the rage. I replied it put me in a rage. She also had on a hat as big as a kitchen coal-scuttle, and the same shape. Mrs. James went home, and both Lupin and I were somewhat pleased—the first time we have agreed on a single subject since his return. Merkins and Son write they have no vacancy for Lupin.

After Pa admitted we agreed on something, there is now a gap of nearly two months in the diary. Pa blamed it all on the mysterious theft of his precious words, but I had my doubts even at the time. I think the fact that I could not find a position and, even worse, that he was not in a position to find me a position, made him fret that he was not such a good father. I also think he wrote harshly in his diary about me, which made him feel better, but then made him feel worse in the event that someone found what he had written and realised he thought his only son was a crinkle-reed. The word is not much used these days – the war has changed slang – but in the 1890s, a crinkle-reed was feckless, hopeless, reckless, and likely to end in the workhouse or to throw himself in front of a train.

My own life changed during those two months – quite dramatically. I fell in love but, naturally, did not tell my parents.

Typically Pa droned on about his diary. No one used the word 'drone' as a verb in 1893. The term was made popular by the success of P.G Wodehouse whose heroes spent days at the Drones club playing cricket, using spuds as balls and pelting each other with bread rolls. If Karl Marx had ever visited Drones, he'd have said that the capitalist class were so bored and degenerate they had nothing better to do. Two months later, two months about which we know little, Pa was no nearer identifying the page thief.

October 30.—I should very much like to know who has wilfully torn the last five or six weeks out of my diary. It is perfectly monstrous! Mine is a large scribbling diary, with plenty of space for the record of my everyday events, and in keeping up that record I take (with much pride) a great deal of pains.

I asked Carrie if she knew anything about it. She replied it was my own fault for leaving the diary about with a charwoman cleaning and the sweeps in the house. I said that was not an answer to my question. This retort of mine, which I thought extremely smart, would have been more effective had I not jogged my elbow against a vase on a table temporarily placed in the passage, knocked it over, and smashed it.

I'm writing after the Great War which saw, among all the other changes, great interest in the new science of psychology. The new-fangled psychologists claim that, when we are anxious and hide from ourselves the reasons for that anxiety, we stumble. We get words wrong or have accidents. The mind is out of kilter and so we knock cups over or get our fingers caught in the mangle. The psychologists didn't do much housework – their chief Sigmund Freud apparently never set foot in his own kitchen – and so they did not see that civilisation has made this problem worse. As we have more and more household devices, we have more and more accidents. An American writer called Thurber believes many car crashes are caused by the fact that the drivers think about girls they would like to poddle, but can't because they imagine sub-consciously their wives are always watching them. The men's minds wander off the steering wheel and they hurtle their cars into the nearest tree.

Pa believed he was anxious because he kept on getting rejections to his pleas for employers to employ me, but it went deeper I think.

October 31.—Received a letter from our principal, Mr. Perkupp, saying that he thinks he knows of a place at last for our dear boy Lupin. This, in a measure, consoles me for the loss of a portion of my diary; for I am bound to confess the last few weeks have been devoted to the record of disappointing answers received from people to whom I have applied for appointments for Lupin. Mrs. Birrell called, and, in reply to me, said: "She never see no book, much less take such a liberty as touch it."

I said I was determined to find out who did it, whereupon she said she would do her best to help me; but she remembered the sweep lighting the fire with a bit of the Echo. I requested the sweep to be sent to me tomorrow.

Pa ended up, of course, blaming me as he had a tendency to do when things were not going his way.

I wish Carrie had not given Lupin a latch-key; we never seem to see anything of him. I sat up till past one for him, and then retired tired.

November 1.—. I would willingly give ten shillings to find out who tore my diary.

I spent the evening quietly with Carrie, of whose company I never tire. We had a most pleasant chat about the letters on "Is Marriage a Failure?" It has been no failure in our case. In talking over our own happy experiences, we never noticed that it was past midnight.

This mention of midnight makes me think thoughts that a son should not think, but thoughts that would not surprise psychologists. Do happy couples not go to bed before midnight so they can make love? Pa does often say they were happy in their marriage but he never gives any intimate details. When I was older, I wondered why I was their only child. Most Victorian families had five or six. Did it mean that, for all their affection, they only poddled – I like the word – like some couples do only on birthdays and Christmas? On this point the diary is silent. Pa just wrote:

We were startled by hearing the door slam violently. Lupin had come in.

I did not slam the door. Pa does exaggerate. Well I was 20 years old and young men have their fancies. I have been completely frank in explaining how I had spent some of my money in Oldham after my win on the horses. I haven't been totally frank though about Sarah, who was not our under-maid, as we could only afford one maid.

Sarah was pretty – and she was, of course, inclined to see the son of the house through rose-tinted spectacles. So I asked her to help me find something I had lost in my room.

"I got you something," I said after I had shut the door.

"Oooh," she said pleased.

"I thought this would look pretty on you."

It was a green necklace that glittered even in the dim light of my bedroom.

"Shall I put it on you?"

"If you like."

I put my hands round her neck and clasped the clasp. She looked at herself in the mirror on my table.

"It looks nice," she grinned.

"You look nice."

"Don't think a nice necklace will get you anything," Sarah said more tartly than I expected. She didn't try to move away though.

"You feel nice too," I said.

"Don't think you can take liberties."

"Of course not." Saying that, I kissed her neck.

"That's a liberty," she pointed out, but she didn't move away. I kissed her ear next.

"That's a big liberty," she laughed, but snuggled against me.

I went on the next liberty. Her breasts felt snug in my hands and I started to caress them.

"Oooh," she purred.

We fell on to my bed.

"Don't make a noise," she whispered, "or I'll be in trouble."

I nodded.

"And don't do that or I'll be in real trouble," she whispered.

Daisy in all her glory

We did, and didn't quite, for an hour when there were footsteps on the stairs. *The Laurels* was a small house in which noises carried.

We were both on our toes at once if you can be on your toes when lying down in a bed. The cistern flushed. *The Laurels* had the luxury of a W.C indoors. More footsteps. Then, the closing of a door.

"I better go back to my room," she said.

Sarah wasn't the kind of girl I wanted, or thought I wanted. I was the son of a seeker after respectability and such men don't marry the maid. I was already walking out with a girl after all, so I thought Sarah was all very well, but maybe I had already found someone better.

When I got home, Pa was out on some mysterious errand too which he did not explain. All he wrote was:

By the time I came home it was 11 p.m.

Lupin made no attempt to turn down the gas in the passage, or even to look into the room where we were, but went straight up to bed, making a terrible noise. I asked him to come down for a moment, and he begged to be excused, as he was "dead beat," an observation that was scarcely consistent with the fact that, for a quarter of an hour afterwards, he was positively dancing in his room, and shouting out, "See me dance the polka!" or some such nonsense.

If Pa came in that late, he had no reason to carp at my twinkle toes. What he also did not say was that Ma came to see me dance too. And Sarah did so too. She gave me a big smile.

"Are you happy about something," Ma asked.

Pa barged in after her and scowled to see me dance. I stopped the polka at once.

"Sarah, you can go to your room now," Ma said not too sternly.

Sarah bobbed a curtsy to Ma and a smile to me.

"Did you get a job," Pa demanded.

"No, I'm dancing because I'm glad to be alive."

"If you don't get a job soon, you'll only polka in the gutter," Pa said sourly.

"Well I expect we all need some sleep," Ma said tactfully and took Pa's arm to steer him back to their bedroom.

"We need to have a talk, boy," Pa said.

"In the morning," Ma said and came to give me a kiss on the cheek.

"Ma," I said. "You used to sing me to sleep."

"I liked doing it," she smiled.

I would have liked her to sing me a song because a mother's voice is comforting.

"Good night dear," she smiled.

"You're too soft on the boy," I heard Pa say from outside the door.

"What's the harm in that?"

I did a few quiet polka steps and then slumped on the bed. I didn't dream. But one of Pa's dreams was coming true.

November 3.—Good news at last. Mr. Perkupp has got an appointment for Lupin, and he is to go and see about it on Monday. Oh, how my mind is relieved! I went to Lupin's room to take the good news to him, but he was in bed, very seedy, so I resolved to keep it over till the evening.

Very seedy indeed ... I was resting after my dramatic exertions which provoked Pa's usual disapproval.

Lupin said he had last night been elected a member of an Amateur Dramatic Club, called the "Holloway Comedians"; and, though it was a pleasant evening, he had sat in a draught, and got neuralgia in the head. He declined to have any breakfast, so I left him.

I suspect Pa was glad my head ached. It was a proper punishment for my dramatics. I should add some history. No one really knows when amateur dramatic clubs started. The Holloway Comedians were the best local club and performed music hall and comedies all over London. I was glad to be involved with them. When Pa got home, he was in a very different mood.

In the evening I had up a special bottle of port, and, Lupin being in for a wonder, we filled our glasses, and I said: "Lupin my boy, I have some good and unexpected news for you. Mr. Perkupp has procured you an appointment!"

I knew that I had to seem happy at that. And that Pa should notice I was noticeably happy.

Lupin said: "Good biz!" and we drained our glasses.

In fact, I did not really think this good at all. I had not met Mr Perkupp, but it seemed likely that he was cut from the same cloth as Mr. Down in Oldham. The truth was, however, that I was down to three pounds. So I said I would be delighted.

"Well you are to come to the office with me Monday." Pa said.

"Excellent biz," I said.

But my true delight was very different as Pa did explain:

Lupin then said: "Fill up the glasses again, for I have some good and unexpected news for you."

I had some slight misgivings, and so evidently had Carrie, for she said: "I hope we shall think it good news."

Lupin said: "Oh, it's all right! I'm engaged to be married!"

It was of course very sudden but young love is sudden. Pa wrote nothing in any detail about my good news and, later, I realised it was because he did not think it too good.

November 5, Sunday.—Carrie and I troubled about that mere boy Lupin getting engaged to be married without consulting us or anything. After dinner he told us all about it. He said the lady's name was Daisy Mutlar, and she was the nicest, prettiest, and most accomplished girl he ever met. He loved her the moment he saw her, and if he had to wait fifty years he would wait, and he knew she would wait for him.

Lupin further said, with much warmth, that the world was a different world to him now,—it was a world worth living in. He lived with an object now, and that was to make Daisy Mutlar—Daisy Pooter, and he would guarantee she would not disgrace the family of the Pooters. Carrie here burst out crying, and threw her arms round his neck, and in doing so, upset the glass of port he held in his hand all over his new light trousers.

I said I had no doubt we should like Miss Mutlar when we saw her, but Carrie said she loved her already. I thought this rather premature, but held my tongue. Daisy Mutlar was the sole topic of conversation for the remainder of the day. I asked Lupin who her people were, and he replied: "Oh, you know Mutlar, Williams and Watts." I did not know, but refrained from asking any further questions at present, for fear of irritating Lupin.

I find this a remarkable admission as my experience was that Pa often couldn't help niggling me. I went to my room and was somewhat surprised to hear a soft knock. I opened it to find Sarah at the door.

"Come in," I said.

"I don't want to now I know you're going to be married."

"Oh."

"I suppose I'm not good enough for you," she started to cry.

"I wasn't engaged when you and I … and I am now."

"I'll tell your ma."

"Please don't."

"Why shouldn't I?"

"I never promised."

"No you just grabbed."

"We didn't..."

"We did enough," she corrected.

"Not the ultimate," I defended myself. I'm not proud of what I did next. I said: "I've got to go with Pa to his office tomorrow. Look why don't you get yourself something nice?"

I gave her a pound which meant my fortune was down to £2.

"You've broken my heart," she cried and tore up the pound note I had just given her.

She slammed the door behind her. Luckily this time neither Pa nor Ma heard. I wonder if Pa had realised I had been tangling with Sarah whether he would have taken me to see Mr Perkupp.

November 6.—Lupin went with me to the office, and had a long conversation with Mr. Perkupp, our principal.

I'd never been to his office in Houndsditch, a name which reminded me of the dog muzzle. Houndsditch was famous for the fact that it had the oldest synagogue in London. Two doors down was a grey building which had been standing for forty or fifty years. It smelled mouldy inside. Pa sat at a kind of elevated desk piled with ledger books – one of a number of middling clerks.

In his diary Pa never described Perkupp but made him out to seem a giant. He was no more than five foot six and he smelt of some lotion. Perhaps he didn't just drink Perk U Uppo but used it as a cologne.

"Ah Mr Pooter junior," he held out his hand. "I am most pleased to meet you. Your father has been diligent for many years and, in fact, he has sat at this desk for the last eight years. Since he rose from being a mere junior clerk."

The mere junior clerks behind Perkupp did their best to smile, having been mired in the mere for years.

"He loves working here," I thought I had better add a deferential, "sir".

"Capital. I have tried to make the experience enjoyable as well as profitable."

"He is devoted, sir, to the interests of the firm and of you personally," I said loudly so Pa could hear.

The niceties done, Perkupp became business-like. "Now young man, can you add up?"

"There is nothing wrong with my numbers, sir."

"And can you subtract?"

"I can plus and minus with the best, sir," I replied.

"Then perhaps you won't mind checking these sums."

"Gladly, sir."

He put a sheet of figures in front of me.

"This desk is free. Make yourself at home." I was very nervous because I did not want to cause Pa problems.

I scooted through the sums, but remembered to check each one before I handed them back to Perkupp.

"I will write to you, Mr Pooter," he said. "I trust there will be no mistakes."

"There will not be," I smiled.

Pa came to see me out. "You were careful I hope, Lupin."

"Very careful, I promise."

I walked out of the building and saw that opposite there was a shop that sold cigars and sherbet lemons. I felt I needed at least a shilling Havana after the calculating ordeal. I needed to calm myself for another reason too. I had not told Pa that I also had been writing round and that I had been asked to see another firm. I thought it would make a good impression to turn up sporting a copy of a new stock paper, *The Investors Chronicle* so I bought one too.

The offices of Job Cleanands and Co., Stock and Share Brokers were much more cheerful than Perkupp's; they had caricatures of London life on the walls. Job Cleanand was about forty years old and, to my surprise, wore a check suit rather like mine Pa had objected to. He asked me to sit down.

"I hope a cigar will put you at your ease," he said.

It was a fat long Havana. He lit one for himself and handed me some matches.

"You should take the paper ring off," he said. "Like this. Now down to brass tacks. You were in a bank. What did you do?"

"I entered the transactions in the ledgers."

"Dull work?"

"Dull but it had to be done."

"Why did you leave the bank? I'd prefer the truth."

"The work was so dull I was disrespectful."

"I did similar work in my youth so I know how dull it is."

"Hardly engages the brain."

"Have you read that copy of *The Investors Chronicle*?"

"Oh yes."

"Then I want you to tell me what shares they recommend – and why?"

I gave a pretty good account of myself.

"You like stocks and shares, I see. The point is can you persuade people to buy them which is what we do here. Stocks they think they can profit from."

The not so sharp life of the clerk

He put a pamphlet in front of me. "Could you improve that?"

"May I have a few minutes?"

"By all means."

The pamphlet touted the merits of Wash It Clean. It was not very snappy so I scribbled:

Your wife washes, your mother washes, your maid washes so Wash it Clean has many customers eager to try it.

"It's not bad, "Job said. "We do need someone to clean up our prose. I'll give you a try."

We agreed I would start two days later. I told Pa in the evening:

"You should have told me."

"I thought you'd be pleased I did it for myself."

"Mr Perkupp found no mistakes."

"I'm not just a calculating machine. And I don't think Perkupp is very up to date."

"Who are you to judge? He's a fine man. I hope you don't regret your folly."

In the diary Pa gave a slightly different account of my view of Cleanands.

Lupin told me, privately, it was an advertising firm, and he did not think much of it. I replied: "Beggars should not be choosers;" and I will do Lupin the justice to say, he looked rather ashamed of himself.

As there were no mirrors handy, I couldn't tell if I looked

rather ashamed. Pa clearly didn't want to dwell on the subject and went to describe how we were going to see fireworks at Cummings' house. But the celebration of finding Guy Fawkes before he blew up Parliament turned out to be no celebration for Pa.

One of my squibs would not go off, and Gowing said: "Hit it on your boot, boy; it will go off then." I gave it a few knocks on the end of my boot, and it went off with one loud explosion, and burnt my fingers rather badly. I gave the rest of the squibs to the little Cummings' boy to let off.

Another unfortunate thing happened, which brought a heap of abuse on my head. Cummings fastened a large wheel set-piece on a stake in the ground by way of a grand finale. He made a great fuss about it; said it cost seven shillings. There was a little difficulty in getting it alight. At last it went off; but after a couple of slow revolutions it stopped. I had my stick with me, so I gave it a tap to send it round, and, unfortunately, it fell off the stake on to the grass. Anybody would have thought I had set the house on fire from the way in which they stormed at me. I will never join in any more firework parties. It is a ridiculous waste of time and money.

That was typical Pa – taking against fireworks because he hadn't worked the fireworks right. I must now say something about Daisy Mutlar to whom I had become engaged. In October, round the time Pa's diary disappeared, I met her at the Holloway Comedians where she sang a number of songs in great style. I congratulated her. She replied I was the most interesting young man she had met for years. For three weeks,

I met her every day. We walked in the park; we lingered in the pub usually till about five in the afternoon when she had to go change for work. Daisy was working in the evenings in a West End restaurant – the Silver Stick. She was, she told me, the head waitress. I asked if I could come to eat there.

"No, I'd end up talking too much to you – and ignoring the real customers," she said.

So I didn't press the point because I didn't want to miff her. Daisy was elegant and she sported or sprouted what Rosie would have called a fine pair. In some ways, she reminded me of Rosie because she was very frank in saying what she liked – and what she didn't.

In 1893, the question of social position obsessed the upper classes, the upper middle classes, the middle classes, the lower middle classes, the lower classes and those who had so little class you could not class them at all. Everyone was frightened of getting it wrong; Pa and Ma were like millions of Victorians. That meant that the question of who invited whom to call on whom was tricky. Etiquette was all.

November 7.—Lupin asked Carrie to call on Mrs. Mutlar, but Carrie said she thought Mrs. Mutlar ought to call on her first. I agreed with Carrie, and this led to an argument. However, the matter was settled by Carrie saying she could not find any visiting cards, and we must get some more printed, and when they were finished would be quite time enough to discuss the etiquette of calling.

November 8.—I ordered some of our cards at Black's, the stationers. I ordered twenty-five of each, which will last us for a good long time. In the evening, Lupin brought in Harry Mutlar,

Miss Mutlar's brother. He was rather a gawky youth, and Lupin said he was the most popular and best amateur in the club, referring to the "Holloway Comedians." Lupin whispered to us that if we could only "draw out" Harry a bit, he would make us roar with laughter.

At supper, young Mutlar did several amusing things. He took up a knife, and with the flat part of it played a tune on his cheek in a wonderful manner. He also gave an imitation of an old man with no teeth, smoking a big cigar. The way he kept dropping the cigar sent Carrie into fits.

In the course of conversation, Daisy's name cropped up, and young Mutlar said he would bring his sister round to us one evening—his parents being rather old-fashioned, and not going out much. Carrie said we would get up a little special party. As young Mutlar showed no inclination to go, and it was approaching eleven o'clock, as a hint I reminded Lupin that he had to be up early tomorrow. Instead of taking the hint, Mutlar began a series of comic imitations. He went on for an hour without cessation. Poor Carrie could scarcely keep her eyes open. At last she made an excuse, and said "Good-night."

Mutlar then left, and I heard him and Lupin whispering in the hall something about the "Holloway Comedians," and to my disgust, although it was past midnight, Lupin put on his hat and coat, and went out with his new companion.

Thank Goodness Pa did not find our true destination. Daisy's brother might look gawky but he was, in fact, a lively lad. He took me to a much smarter place than Caldwell's. I decided that after my adventures with Sarah and now being engaged, I shouldn't do anything other than dance. Still, being young, I found myself asking a redhead to dance. She reminded me of Rosie in Oldham.

"Is it just your feet you know how to use," she said, pressing herself against me.

"I'm afraid I'm engaged."

"Even being married doesn't stop most men."

"I'm trying to turn over a new leaf."

For a moment I nearly succumbed, but then I decided New Leaf Lupin would behave in a very proper manner. The red head deliberately trod on my left foot.

"I'm sorry I bothered to dance with you," she snapped as she went off in search of a partner who might be more footloose and fancy free.

I left a few minutes later. When I got home I found Pa had taken all the cushions off the sofa and was searching inside.

"What are you doing?"

"They must be somewhere," he shouted at me. "Things don't just disappear."

Pa was still obsessing about the lost pages of his diary.

November 9.—My endeavours to discover who tore the sheets out of my diary still fruitless. Lupin has Daisy Mutlar on the brain, so we see little of him, except that he invariably turns up at meal times. Cummings dropped in.

November 10.—Lupin seems to like his new berth—that's a comfort. Daisy Mutlar the sole topic of conversation during tea. Carrie almost as full of it as Lupin. Lupin informs me, to my disgust, that he has been persuaded to take part in the forthcoming performance of the "Holloway Comedians." He says he is to play Bob Britches in the farce, Gone to my Uncle's; Frank Mutlar is going to play old Musty. I told Lupin pretty plainly I was not in the least degree interested in the matter, and totally disapproved of amateur theatricals.

Why did Pa disapprove so much of amateur theatricals? Because they were not respectable and he was trying hard to make himself respectable and, therefore, worthy of Perkupp.

Pa went to bed early as he had to prepare for the great event in his social calendar.

November 11.—Everybody so far has accepted for our quite grand little party for tomorrow. Mr. Perkupp, in a nice letter which I shall keep, wrote that he was dining in Kensington, but if he could get away, he would come up to Holloway for an hour. Carrie was busy all day, making little cakes and open jam puffs and jellies. She said she felt quite nervous about her responsibilities tomorrow evening. We decided to have some light things on the table, such as sandwiches, cold chicken and ham, and some sweets, and on the sideboard a nice piece of cold beef and a Paysandu tongue—for the more hungry ones to peg into if they liked.

People now may not know what a Paysandu tongue was. So here is all you need to find out.

In the 1800s ox tongue was considered a great luxury, sometimes it was stewed which made it very soft, other times it was pickled and the added salt made it extremely hard. It was often served at Buckingham Palace apparently. Pa had talked up the party as if it was a royal event.

Gowing called to know if he was to put on "swallow-tails" tomorrow. Carrie said he had better dress, especially as Mr. Franching was coming, and there was a possibility of Mr. Perkupp also putting in an appearance.

Gowing said: "Oh, I only wanted to know, for I have not worn my dress-coat for some time, and I must send it to have the creases pressed out."

After Gowing left, Lupin came in, and in his anxiety to please Daisy Mutlar, carped at and criticised the arrangements, and, in fact, disapproved of everything, including our having asked our old friend Cummings, who, he said, would look in evening-dress like a green-grocer engaged to wait, and who must not be surprised if Daisy took him for one.

I fairly lost my temper, and said: "Lupin, allow me to tell you Miss Daisy Mutlar is not the Queen of England. I gave you credit for more wisdom than to allow yourself to be inveigled into an engagement with a woman considerably older than yourself. I advise you to think of earning your living before entangling yourself with a wife whom you will have to support, and, in all probability, her brother also, who appeared to be nothing but a loafer."

Instead of receiving this advice in a sensible manner, Lupin jumped up and said: "If you insult the lady I am engaged to, you insult me. I will leave the house and never darken your doors again." He went out of the house, slamming the hall-door.

I can now see my reaction was somewhat excessive. One of the reasons I left in a huff was that in some part of what is now called my unconscious mind I did wonder if Pa might not be right – and that Daisy might not be perfection itself.

I walked down to the Holloway Road and went into the Queen of Denmark where I calmed myself with a whisky. Having downed two, I walked back and apologised. I was mature enough to do that but you'd never have guessed it from the diary. Pa just said:

But it was all right. He came back to supper, and we played Bézique till nearly twelve o'clock.

I went up to my room after that and got into my pyjamas. I lit a small cigar and was drifting off when Sarah knocked at the door. I did not want to see her.

"I've got a headache," I tried to put her off.

That didn't stop her.

"Is that a way for a young man to talk to a young lady? You're in the spot you like best – bed."

"I'm sorry. What do you want?"

"Aren't you pleased to see me," she sat most familiarly on the side of my bed.

"It's late and I've got a head like a melon."

"Do melons get sore heads? Don't think so," Sarah laughed. I laughed back a little nervously.

"If I laugh it makes my head worse."

"Serves you right." She became more serious. "I'm not sure I can stand you being engaged to this Daisy. What does she have that I don't? Does she make you laugh?"

"Sarah," I said.

"Does she do this better than I do?"

She kissed me rather enticingly – but just at that moment Ma walked in.

"I thought I heard voices," Ma said quietly.

"I'm very sorry," Sarah leapt off the bed.

"I'm very sorry," I said too.

"I'm very sorry," Ma said too, "and everyone will be even sorrier if your Pa finds out."

"Finds out what," I affected innocence.

"You better go Sarah," Ma said softly, but not softly enough.

"What's going on here," Pa said. There were now four people in my small room.

Ma was up to the crisis. "Sarah and I heard Lupin cry out and we came to see what was wrong."

"I was having a nightmare," I put my hands up to my head to look like I had been suffering.

"Mothers are good with nightmares," Ma added.

"When I heard him cry out, I thought Lupin might want some beef tea," Sarah added for her part.

"Mr Lupin to you. We're not communists here. And I see no beef tea," Pa said.

"Sarah came to ask if he might want some. I'll look after him, Charlie," Ma said firmly. "You acted kindly Sarah. I won't forget it. You go to bed now. You too, Charlie."

When Ma was firm, Pa usually did what she wanted.

The moment the two of them had gone, Ma sat on the bed.

"Nightmares? More like night jinks. You better tell your ma what you've been up to."

I spluttered because I didn't want to say.

"It's no good having secrets from your ma – and I can guess anyway."

"I only kissed her, ma." Which of course was not the whole truth but mothers don't need too much detail.

"She's our maid," Ma said. "One kiss is too much. Not to mention you being engaged to someone else."

"I won't do it again," I promised.

"You better not. She's sweet on you. I'll deal with it."

Ma got up and left.

I didn't find it easy to get to sleep because Sarah had been quite enticing – and when young men are enticed, they don't just drift off to sleep when they are left alone. It must have been very late when I finally drifted off.

For Pa the party was to be a great moment so I will let him describe it. But first I better correct an error. He says I had made three pounds in a private deal. I had in fact made six but I didn't dare tell Pa who wouldn't have been listening anyway because his mind was on the party.

A red-letter day. Our first important party since we have been in this house. I got home early from the City. Lupin insisted on having a hired waiter, and stood a half-dozen of champagne. I think this an unnecessary expense, but Lupin said he had had a piece of luck, having made three pounds out a private deal in the City. I hope he won't gamble in his new situation. The supper-room looked so nice, and Carrie truly said: "We need not be ashamed of its being seen by Mr. Perkupp, should he honour us by coming."

For Pa a visit by the Queen would be less important than a visit by Mr Perkupp. I vowed then that I would not to be so in thrall to any employer as Pa was to his. Pa might as well have been a mediaeval serf. He spent the whole day worrying about the arrangements which had to be perfect as Perfect Perkupp would honour us with his perfect presence. Alas one flaw in the perfection; Pa's trousers were letting him down.

I dressed early in case people should arrive punctually at eight o'clock, and was much vexed to find my new dress-trousers much too short.

Lupin, who is getting beyond his position, found fault with my wearing ordinary boots instead of dress-boots.

I replied satirically: "My dear son, I have lived to be above that sort of thing."

Lupin burst out laughing, and said: "A man generally was above his boots."

This may be funny, or it may not; but I was gratified to find he had not discovered the coral had come off one of my studs. Carrie looked a picture, wearing the dress she wore at the Mansion House. The arrangement of the drawing-room was excellent. Carrie had hung muslin curtains over the folding-doors, and also over one of the entrances, for we had removed the door from its hinges.

Mr. Peters, the waiter, arrived in good time, and I gave him strict orders not to open another bottle of champagne until the previous one was empty.

I was determined to impress Daisy and her family so when I overheard Pa whispering to Peters, I took the man to one side and gave him a pound and ten shillings to buy four more bottles. I told Pa what I had done.

"You can only do that because you have been living off the fat of my land for months," he complained.

"I want the party to be what you hope, Pa."

Pa was too frazzled by whether everything was Perkupp Perfect to reply. He went to check the champagne and Sarah came up beside me.

"What you want is not to be found out. It's a good thing for you that I like your Ma or I'd tell the whole truth," Sarah said.

"Thank you. Really. You know how much this means to him."

To my surprise, she squeezed my hand.

To my surprise, I squeezed hers.

A few minutes later Peters came back with bottles and smiled at Sarah. He was much taken with her. He blushed when she was by his side. Sarah patted him on the arm as one pats a dog and left him to set the champagne out. Pa was like a nervous hawk who hadn't caught sparrow for a while, eyeing everything.

Carrie arranged for some sherry and port wine to be placed on the drawing-room sideboard, with some glasses. By-the-by, our new enlarged and tinted photographs look very nice on the walls, especially as Carrie has arranged some Liberty silk bows on the four corners of them.

The first arrival was Gowing, who, with his usual taste, greeted me with: "Hulloh, Pooter, why your trousers are too short!"

I simply said: "Very likely, and you will find my temper 'short' also."

Gowing, Pa and friends playing one of their games

He said: "That won't make your trousers longer, Juggins. You should get your missus to put a flounce on them."

I wonder I waste my time entering his insulting observations in my diary.

Pa entered his insulting observations because he was always nervous. He did not know the truth about Gowing, but he somehow realised the man was not a wage slave as he was and that gave him a breezy self-confidence. God knows what Gowing would have been like if he had owned a whole shop.

The next arrivals were Mr. and Mrs. Cummings. The former said: "As you didn't say anything about dress, I have come 'half dress.'" He had on a black frock-coat and white tie. The James', Mr. Merton, and Mr. Stillbrook arrived, but Lupin was restless and unbearable till his Daisy Mutlar and Frank arrived.

Carrie and I were rather startled at Daisy's appearance. She had a bright-crimson dress on, cut very low in the neck. I do not think such a style modest. She ought to have taken a lesson from Carrie, and covered her shoulders with a little lace.

I have described earlier how beautiful I found Daisy so when I read what Pa said about her I was hurt. Now I realise that he was frightened because she was noticeable.

Mr. Nackles, Mr. Sprice-Hogg and his four daughters came; so did Franching, and one or two of Lupin's new friends, members of the "Holloway Comedians." Some of these seemed rather theatrical in their manner, especially one, who was posing all the evening, and leant on our little round table and cracked it. Lupin called him "our Henry," and said he was "our lead at the H.C.'s," and was quite as good in that department as Harry Mutlar was as the low-comedy merchant. All this is Greek to me.

Pa simply didn't understand why the drama interested me, but he could not resist some sort of joke. He affected not to understand all the theatricals but then added it was "Greek", like a Greek tragedy. I've always dreamed of writing Oedipus in the suburbs.

I must confess Daisy was also upsetting me. As soon as the comedians arrived, she started flirting with one of them.

"She's an old trout, and welcome to you," Sarah whispered to me, and added even lower. "And does she know the tongue tricks I do?"

"Marriage isn't just tongue tricks," I told her, sticking out my tongue.

"It's better tricks too," she laughed. "If I can make your tongue tingle, just think what I could to some of your other bits."

To my horror in the middle of the party, my other bits perked up.

"I can't just stand here frivolling with you," I said.

"Daisy wouldn't like it," Sarah stalked off.

Luckily, Pa didn't see any of this. He wrote:

We had some music, and Lupin, who never left Daisy's side for a moment, raved over her singing of a song, called "Some Day." It seemed a pretty song, but she made such grimaces, and sang, to my mind, so out of tune, I would not have asked her to sing again; but Lupin made her sing four songs right off, one after the other.

Daisy looked into my eyes, and sang:

Some day
I will love you forever
Some day
Oh yes I will never
Love another
Love your brother
Cause you bother
No way.

I found her singing very lovely and told her so.

"People have always said I had a lovely voice," she smiled. "Soon I'll give up being a waitress and sing professionally."

"You will," I said.

"I expect you to help. But I can't sing another note till I eat. Artistes have appetites," Daisy said.

Ma had become anxious that we had not fed our guests and nudged Pa to announced supper.

At ten o'clock we went down to supper, and from the way Gowing and Cummings ate you would have thought they had not had a meal for a month. I told Carrie to keep something back in case Mr. Perkupp should come by mere chance. Gowing annoyed me very much by filling a large tumbler of champagne, and drinking it straight off. He repeated this action, and made me fear our half-dozen of champagne would not last out. I tried to keep a bottle back, but Lupin got hold of it, and took it to the side-table with Daisy and Frank Mutlar.

We went upstairs, and the young fellows began skylarking. Carrie put a stop to that at once. Stillbrook amused us with a song, "What have you done with your Cousin John?" I did not notice that Lupin and Frank had disappeared. I asked Mr. Watson, one of the Holloways, where they were, and he said: "It's a case of 'Oh, what a surprise!'"

We were directed to form a circle—which we did. Watson then said: "I have much pleasure in introducing the celebrated Blondin Donkey." Frank and Lupin then bounded into the room. Lupin had whitened his face like a clown, and Frank had tied round his waist a large hearthrug. He was supposed to be the donkey, and he looked it. They indulged in a very noisy pantomime, and we were all shrieking with laughter.

I was having a whale of a time if a donkey can have a whale of a time.

Even Sarah and Peters were shrieking with laughter. In grand houses the servants may be left to wait below, skulking in the scullery, but *The Laurels* did not have a basement, so the 'servants' were upstairs with the rest of us.

But then the calamity because the great I am arrived and startled Pa.

I turned round suddenly, and then I saw Mr. Perkupp standing half-way in the door, he having arrived without our knowing it. I beckoned to Carrie, and we went up to him at once. He would not come right into the room. I apologised for the foolery, but Mr. Perkupp said: "Oh, it seems amusing." I could see he was not a bit amused.

Mr Perkupp

It never occurred to Pa to ask why his saintly employer turned up so late. Perkupp had clearly had more than a skinful at his dinner in Kensington and was not so much standing up as lurching and finally sat down. Pa smiled at him sycophantically. Later on I would discover where Perkupp might have been – and it wasn't tucking into beef and oysters in Kensington.

Carrie and I took him downstairs, but the table was a wreck. There was not a glass of champagne left—not even a sandwich. Mr. Perkupp said he required nothing, but would like a glass of seltzer or soda water. The last syphon was empty. Carrie said: "We have plenty of port wine left." Mr. Perkupp said, with a smile: "No, thank you. I really require nothing, but I am most pleased to see you and your husband in your own home. Good-night, Mrs. Pooter—you will excuse my very short stay, I know." I went with him to his carriage, and he said: "Don't trouble to come to the office till twelve tomorrow."

I felt despondent as I went back to the house, and I told Carrie I thought the party was a failure. Carrie said it was a great success, and I was only tired, and insisted on my having some port myself. I drank two glasses, and felt much better, and we went into the drawing-room, where they had commenced dancing. Carrie and I had a little dance, which I said reminded me of old days. She said I was a spooney old thing

Pa did have a sentimental streak.

November 16.—The many changes in my life have made me aware of my inner life, a diabolo the new psychologists often talk about. You may not have heard of the word 'diabolo' but it comes from devil. Pa does not often talk about his inner life and, indeed, he may not have realised he had one. But he was clearly troubled and just like the psychologists predicted, his worries surfaced in his dreams.

Woke about twenty times during the night, with terrible thirst. Finished off all the water in the bottle, as well as half that in the jug. Kept dreaming also, that last night's party was a failure, and that a lot of low people came without invitation, and kept chaffing and throwing things at Mr. Perkupp, till at last I was obliged to hide him in the box-room (which we had just discovered), with a bath-towel over him. It seems absurd now, but it was painfully real in the dream. I had the same dream about a dozen times.

Pa had no idea of the latest theories about dreams then or, honestly, ever. Dreams are wish fulfilments, the psychologists say. And often reveal wishes we dare not admit, of which the most distressing are hostile and the nice ones most unlikely to happen. The key thing about Pa's dream was he was not the vicious and ungrateful person to throw things at the spotless Perkupp, it was a lot of 'low people' who had not even been invited into the coal store. When these events happened I could not have begun to understand the truth but more than 20 years on I can. Pa could never admit he wanted to throw things at Perkupp so it was someone else who did that in his dream. The attack allowed Pa to pose as Perkupp's saviour, but even that rescue was not totally benign. Pa locked the Supreme Being in the box room and threw a bath towel over him so Perkupp would find it hard to breathe. In other words the dream really meant that, after 21 years of lick spittling in the ledgers, Pa wanted to throw things at Perkupp and stop him breathing. The truth will out in dreams. In fact Pa really hated him, a terrifying thought quite at odds with what he believed. So he had to repress it, as the mind scientists say these days.

I did not have the insight to realise this in 1893, but now I can imagine the conversation we might have had.

"Don't you see what this means, Pa?"

"We have to put better locks so people can't turn up uninvited."

"No, it tells you something about your feelings about Perkupp."

"I admire him as you know," Pa said. "The best of men."

"You think he's the best of men and you admire him, Pa but in your unconscious mind he evokes less lovely feelings."

"I don't have an unconscious mind," Pa replied.

"It frightens you, Pa. It frightens most men. That's why it's unconscious."

"Is that the new slang, Lupin?"

"No, it's the new science."

"As usual you don't know what you're talking about."

"He is your slave driver, Pa and slaves hate their slave drivers, even though they sometimes don't know it."

"Slave? Mr Perkupp has never whipped me or put me in chains," Pa said with dignity.

In the privacy of their bedroom Pa seems to have told Ma his dream and, as so often, she did try to cheer him up by putting it all down to bubbles.

Carrie annoyed me by saying: "You know champagne never agrees with you." I told her I had only a couple of glasses of it, having kept myself entirely to port. I added that good champagne hurt nobody, and Lupin told me he had only got it from a traveller as a favour, as that particular brand had been entirely bought up by a West-End club.

I think I ate too heartily of the "side dishes," as the waiter called them. I said to Carrie: "I wish I had put those 'side dishes' aside."

Yet another of Pa's puns!

But Carrie was busy, packing up the teaspoons we had borrowed of Mrs. Cummings for the party. It was just half-past eleven, and I was starting for the office, when Lupin appeared, with a yellow complexion, and said: "Hulloh! Guv., what priced head have you this morning?" I told him he might just as well speak to me in Dutch. He added: "When I woke this morning, my head was as big as Baldwin's balloon." On the spur of the moment I said the cleverest thing I think I have ever said: viz.: "Perhaps that accounts for the parashooting pains." We roared.

Even I roared because as I said Pa did sometimes hit the nail.

I don't know what Pa dreamed of that night, but it did him good.

November 18.—Woke up quite fresh after a good night's rest, and feel quite myself again. I am satisfied a life of going-out and

Society is not a life for me; we therefore declined the invitation which we received this morning to Miss Bird's wedding. We only met her twice at Mrs. James', and it means a present. Lupin said: "I am with you for once. To my mind a wedding's a very poor play. There are only two parts in it—the bride and bridegroom. The best man is only a walking gentleman. With the exception of a crying father and a snivelling mother, the rest are supers who have to dress well and have to pay for their insignificant parts in the shape of costly presents." I did not care for the theatrical slang, but thought it clever, though disrespectful.

I told Sarah not to bring up the blanc-mange again for breakfast. It seems to have been placed on our table at every meal since Wednesday. Cummings came round in the evening, and congratulated us on the success of our party. He said it was the best party he had been to for many a year; but he wished we had let him know it was full dress, as he would have turned up in his swallow-tails. We sat down to a quiet game of dominoes, and were interrupted by the noisy entrance of Lupin and Frank Mutlar. Cummings and I asked them to join us. Lupin said he did not care for dominoes, and suggested a game of "Spoof." On my asking if it required counters, Frank and Lupin in measured time said: "One, two, three; go! Have you an estate in Greenland?" It was simply Greek to me, but it appears it is one of the customs of the "Holloway Comedians" to do this when a member displays ignorance.

In spite of my instructions, that blancmange was brought up again for supper. To make matters worse, there had been an attempt to disguise it, by placing it in a glass dish with jam round it. Carrie asked Lupin if he would have some, and he replied: "No second-hand goods for me, thank you." I told Carrie, when we were alone, if that blanc-mange were placed on the table again I should walk out of the house.

The question is: do you blame me for being waspish or praise Pa for being so honest about being driven to such extreme feelings by a bland dessert? Pa got over his dessert distress quickly, however, and was able to enjoy everything else on the table.

November 19, Sunday.—A delightfully quiet day.

In the afternoon Lupin was off to spend the rest of the day with the Mutlars. He departed in the best of spirits, and Carrie said: "Well, one advantage of Lupin's engagement with Daisy is that the boy seems happy all day long. That quite reconciles me to what I must confess seems an imprudent engagement."

The morning was delightfully quiet for Pa as I had a lie in and then went out to buy *The Sunday Pictorial.* My day at the Mutlars was less quiet. Daisy was not in. She had apparently gone to church which surprised me, as I did not take her for a pew girl. But it turned out there were many things I did not realise about her. Old man Mutlar was smoking a pipe in his living room. Daisy's brother Frank suggested that we read a scene from a play together. As soon as we started, Mr Mutlar groused that if he wanted to be subjected to theatricals, he would go to the theatre.

"You are making a fog with your pipe, dad," his son Frank said.

"It's my house and I'll fog it up if I please," his father replied.

When Daisy came back, she suggested we go to the Oyster and Fiddle as she did not want to be cooped up all day in a pipe souper. I now have got Pa's pun mania. Fogs were known as pea soupers so you see where I got pipe souper from.

We walked to the pub – and our own Waterloo. Pa meanwhile enjoyed the peace in his house.

Carrie and I talked the matter over and agreed that it did not always follow that an early engagement meant an unhappy marriage. Dear Carrie reminded me that we married early, and, with the exception of a few trivial misunderstandings, we had never had a really serious word. I could not help thinking (as I told her) that half the pleasures of life were derived from the little struggles and small privations that one had to endure at the beginning of one's married life. Such struggles were generally occasioned by want of means, and often helped to make loving couples stand together all the firmer.

Carrie said I had expressed myself wonderfully well, and that I was quite a philosopher.

We are all vain at times, and I must confess I felt flattered by Carrie's little compliment. I don't pretend to be able to express myself in fine language, but I feel I have the power of expressing my thoughts with simplicity and lucidness. About nine o'clock, to our surprise, Lupin entered, with a wild, reckless look, and in a hollow voice, which I must say seemed rather theatrical, said: "Have you any brandy?" I said: "No; but here is some whisky." Lupin drank off nearly a wineglassful without water, to my horror.

We all three sat reading in silence till ten, when Carrie and I rose to go to bed. Carrie said to Lupin: "I hope Daisy is well?"

Lupin, with a forced careless air that he must have picked up from the "Holloway Comedians," replied: "Oh, Daisy? You mean Miss Mutlar. I don't know whether she is well or not, but please never to mention her name again in my presence."

I better explain what had led to the rupture. I have been honest in describing my encounters with Rosie and with Sarah. Daisy was a cut above them and I rather liked the fact that she was high and haughty. By the time we left the pub it was evening and dark because one of London's usual pea soupers had settled on the streets. We were walking back affectionately arm in arm from the Oyster and Fiddle when I stopped and turned to face her. I brought my lips close to hers.

"I don't like kissing much," Daisy said.

I was shocked.

"Though once we are married, I'll give it a try."

I wanted to say "that's big of you".

Then she took my hands on put them on her breasts.

"And I find this tickles so don't expect nights of passion."

"What's wrong with nights of passion?"

"They mess your hair," she said.

"You can always do your hair again."

"A woman's hair is her glory. Boys like you have no idea how long it takes to do it right."

I began to fret that being married to Daisy might lead to many nights when it was rather more than my hair that was messed up.

She slipped out of my arms. "Do you snore," she said.

"Only on Tuesdays," I said as I was now peeved.

"The smallest noise bothers me when I sleep."

"I could always sleep with a nose peg on."

"You can put a peg on your peg too," she laughed.

"I'm sure I can persuade you kissing and more can be fun."

"I'm sure I can persuade the Queen to bat against W.G Grace," Daisy snipped back.

"I'm a little surprised by your dislike of kissing."

"Like all beastly men you just want one beastly thing," Daisy said.

"I want at least three things." I whispered what the two beyond kissing were.

"Well I don't, and you shouldn't mention such things to a respectable girl," she said. And walked away.

"Daisy," I ran after her.

"Don't you Daisy me," she said as she kept on walking. "You're just interested in getting my knickers off," she shouted.

Luckily because of the pea souper, no one could see who she was shouting at.

I got back home, said a curt good night to Ma and Pa and went to bed.

By the time I got up the next day, Pa had gone to work. I went for a long walk and wondered whether I should call on Daisy but decided not to.

November 21.—Lupin turned up for a few minutes in the evening. He asked for a drop of brandy with a sort of careless look, which to my mind was theatrical and quite ineffective. I said: "My boy, I have none, and I don't think I should give it you if I had." Lupin said: "I'll go where I can get some," and walked out of the house. Carrie took the boy's part, and the rest of the evening was spent in a disagreeable discussion, in which the words "Daisy" and "Mutlar" must have occurred a thousand times.

I couldn't of course say why Daisy and I had fought even though Pa kept asking.

"If you don't tell us, we have to assume you upset her," Pa added.

November 22.—Gowing and Cummings dropped in during the evening. Lupin also came in, bringing his friend, Mr. Burwin-Fosselton—one of the "Holloway Comedians"—who was at our party the other night, and who cracked our little round table. Happy to say Daisy Mutlar was never referred to. The conversation was almost entirely monopolised by the young fellow Fosselton, who not only looked rather like Mr. Irving, but seemed to imagine that he was the celebrated actor. I must say he gave some capital imitations of him. As he showed no signs of moving at supper time, I said: "If you like to stay, Mr. Fosselton, for our usual crust—pray do." He replied: "Oh! thanks; but please call me Burwin-Fosselton. It is a double name. There are lots of Fosseltons, but please call me Burwin-Fosselton."

He began doing the Irving business all through supper. He sank so low down in his chair that his chin was almost on a level with the table, and twice he kicked Carrie under the table, upset his wine, and flashed a knife uncomfortably near Gowing's face. After supper he kept stretching out his legs on the fender, indulging in scraps of quotations from plays which were Greek to me, and more than once knocked over the fire-irons, making a hideous row—poor Carrie already having a bad headache.

When he went, he said, to our surprise: "I will come tomorrow and bring my Irving make-up." Gowing and Cummings said they would like to see it and would come too. I could not help thinking they might as well give a party at my house while they are about it. However, as Carrie sensibly said: "Do anything, dear, to make Lupin forget the Daisy Mutlar business."

Henry Irving was one of the great actors of the day. He started with the Lyceum Theatre in 1871 and helped restore its fortunes with his Mathias in *The Bells*. Three years later his unconventional Hamlet caused another sensation. In 1875, he played Macbeth and a year later Othello. One curiosity – since reading leads you to find them. Irving became lifelong friends with Bram Stoker, the author of *Dracula*, who praised his *Hamlet*. He wanted Irving to change the great soliloquy to "to fang or not to fang, that is the question." Not really. Stoker had decent taste.

In 1878, Irving entered into a partnership with the actress Ellen Terry and re-opened the Lyceum under his own management. The two were lovers almost certainly. Fifteen years later, Irving still ruled the London stage and was admired, loved, hated and imitated. Especially by amateurs.

November 23.—In the evening, Cummings came early. Gowing came a little later and brought, without asking permission, a fat and, I think, very vulgar-looking man named Padge, who appeared to be all moustache. Gowing never attempted any apology to either of us, but said Padge wanted to see the Irving business, to which Padge said: "That's right," and that is about all he did say during the entire evening. Lupin came

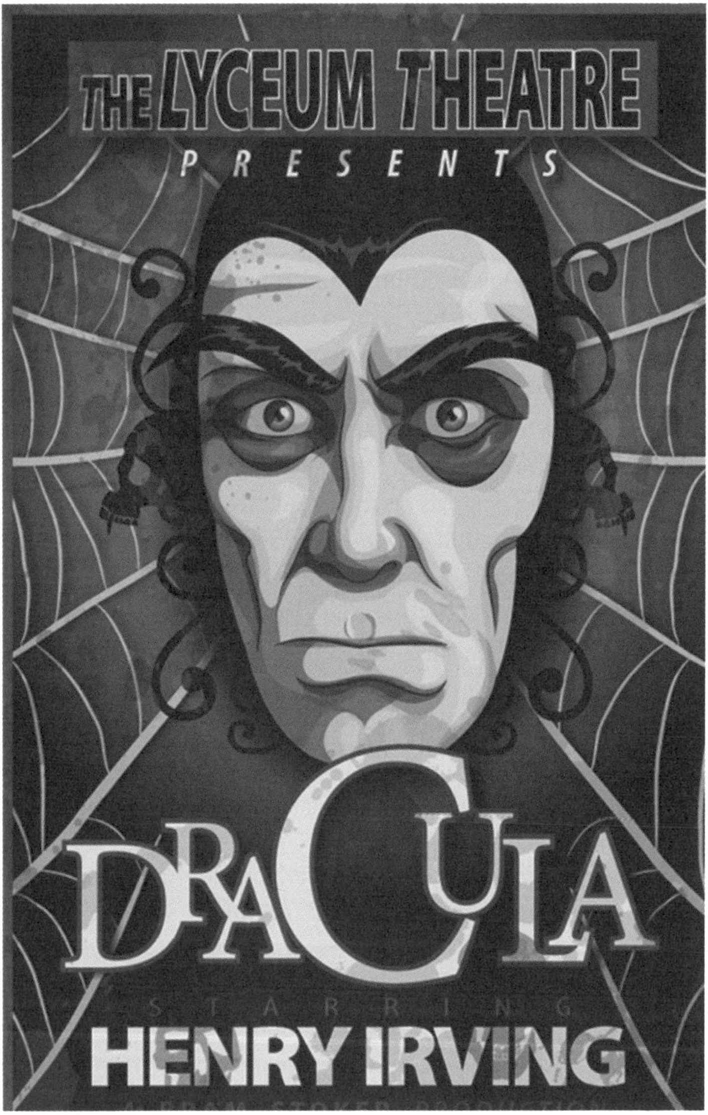
THE LYCEUM THEATRE
PRESENTS
DRACULA
STARRING
HENRY IRVING

in and seemed in much better spirits. He had prepared a bit of a surprise. Mr. Burwin-Fosselton had come in with him, but had gone upstairs to get ready. In half-an-hour Lupin retired from the parlour, and returning in a few minutes, announced "Mr. Henry Irving."

I must say we were all astounded. I never saw such a resemblance. It was astonishing. The only person who did not appear interested was the man Padge, who had got the best arm-chair, and was puffing away at a foul pipe into the fireplace. After some little time I said: "Why do actors always wear their hair so long?" Carrie in a moment said, "Mr. Hare doesn't wear long hair." How we laughed except Mr. Fosselton, who said, in a rather patronising kind of way, "The joke, Mrs. Pooter, is extremely appropriate, if not altogether new." Thinking this rather a snub, I said: "Mr. Fosselton, I fancy—" He interrupted me by saying: "Mr. Burwin-Fosselton, if you please," which made me quite forget what I was going to say to him. During the supper Mr. Burwin-Fosselton again monopolised the conversation with his Irving talk, and both Carrie and I came to the conclusion one can have even too much imitation of Irving. After supper, Mr. Burwin-Fosselton got a little too boisterous over his Irving imitation, and suddenly seizing Gowing by the collar of his coat, dug his thumb-nail, accidentally of course, into Gowing's neck and took a piece of flesh out. Gowing was rightly annoyed, but that man Padge, who having declined our modest supper in order that he should not lose his comfortable chair, burst into an uncontrollable fit of laughter at the little misadventure. I was so annoyed at the conduct of Padge, I said: "I suppose you would have laughed if he had poked Mr. Gowing's eye out?" to which Padge replied: "That's right," and laughed more than ever. I think

Padge in his comfortable chair

perhaps the greatest surprise was when we broke up, for Mr. Burwin-Fosselton said: "Good-night, Mr. Pooter. I'm glad you like the imitation, I'll bring the other make-up tomorrow night."

November 25.—Had a long letter from Mr. Fosselton respecting last night's Irving discussion. I was very angry, and I wrote and said I knew little or nothing about stage matters, was not in the least interested in them and positively declined to be drawn into a discussion on the subject, even at the risk of its leading to a breach of friendship. I never wrote a more determined letter.

On returning home at the usual hour on Saturday afternoon I met near the Archway Daisy Mutlar. My heart gave a leap. I bowed rather stiffly, but she affected not to have seen me.

Was he telling the truth about meeting Daisy or was he just having a critical go? The other possibility is that he imagined seeing her as he had his own fantasies about her. The new psychology teaches us fathers may have all kinds of fantasies about girls their sons love. Pa did not elaborate and, instead, ignoring his own unconscious as usual, focussed on socks – a word which in English rhymes with a part of a sexual nature. I don't know if socks in French, Italian or German rhymes with a rude word too.

Very much annoyed in the evening by the laundress sending home an odd sock. Sarah said she sent two pairs, and the laundress declared only a pair and a half were sent. I spoke to Carrie about it, but she rather testily replied: "I am tired of speaking to her; you had better go and speak to her yourself. She is outside." I did so, but the laundress declared that only an odd sock was sent.

Gowing passed into the passage at this time and was rude enough to listen to the conversation, and interrupting, said: "Don't waste the odd sock, old man; do an act of charity and give it to some poor man with only one leg." The laundress giggled like an idiot. I was disgusted and walked upstairs for the purpose of pinning down my collar, as the button had come off the back of my shirt.

When I returned to the parlour, Gowing was retailing his idiotic joke about the odd sock, and Carrie was roaring with laughter. I suppose I am losing my sense of humour. I spoke my mind pretty freely about Padge. Gowing said he had met him only once before that evening. He had been introduced by a friend, and as he (Padge) had "stood" a good dinner, Gowing wished to show him some little return. Upon my word, Gowing's coolness surpasses all belief.

The truth was that Pa and Ma did not own anything apart from their clothes, some of the crockery and modest savings. They were typical of what we now call the lower middle-class – the working not quite poor.

Lupin came in before I could reply, and Gowing unfortunately inquired after Daisy Mutlar. Lupin shouted: "Mind your own business, sir!" and bounced out of the room, slamming the door.

The remainder of the night was Daisy Mutlar—Daisy Mutlar—Daisy Mutlar. Oh dear!

I probably should not have shouted, but a man doesn't like being made to seem ridiculous in front of his father's friends so I understand why I did, but I still shouldn't have. My excuse is that I was still rattled by Daisy's coldness. I felt I had to say something, but I found myself tongue tied so I took refuge in being grumpy. Pa could not fail to notice. I might as well add that I did not go church the next day, and so missed a sermon that apparently St Paul himself would have been proud of preaching. For Pa church was a social occasion as he made clear when he highlighted his talk with Mrs Fernlosse.

November 26, Sunday.—The curate preached a very good sermon to-day—very good indeed. His appearance is never so impressive as our dear old vicar's, but I am bound to say his sermons are much more impressive. A rather annoying incident occurred, of which I must make mention. Mrs. Fernlosse, who is quite a grand lady, living in one of those large houses in the Camden Road, stopped to speak to me after church, when we were all coming out. I must say I felt flattered, for she is thought a good deal of. I suppose she knew me through seeing me so often take round the plate, especially as she always occupies the corner seat of the pew. She is a very influential lady, and may have had something of the utmost importance to say, but unfortunately, as she commenced to speak a strong gust of wind came and blew my hat off into the middle of the road.

I had to run after it, and had the greatest difficulty in recovering it. When I had succeeded in doing so, I found Mrs. Fernlosse had walked on with some swell friends, and I felt I could not well approach her now, especially as my hat was smothered with mud. I cannot say how disappointed I felt.

In the evening (Sunday evening of all others) I found an impertinent note from Mr. Burwin-Fosselton, which ran as follows:

"DEAR MR. POOTER,—Although your junior by perhaps some twenty or thirty years—which is sufficient reason that you ought to have a longer record of the things and ways in this miniature of a planet—I feel it is just within the bounds of possibility that the wheels of your life don't travel so quickly round as those of the humble writer of these lines. The dandy horse of past days has been known to overtake the slow coach.

"Do I make myself understood?

"Very well, then! Permit me, Mr. Pooter, to advise you to accept the verb. sap. Acknowledge your defeat, and take your whipping gracefully; for remember you threw down the glove, and I cannot claim to be either mentally or physically a coward!

"Revenons à nos moutons.

Return to our muttons is French slang, for let's get back

to the point. What muttons have to do with keeping to the point I don't know, but it shows how odd the French can be.

"Our lives run in different grooves. I live for MY ART—THE STAGE. Your life is devoted to commercial pursuits—'A life among Ledgers.' My books are of different metal. Your life in the City is honourable, I admit. But how different! Cannot even you see the ocean between us? A channel that prevents the meeting of our brains in harmonious accord. Ah! But chaçun à son goût.

"I have registered a vow to mount the steps of fame. I may crawl, I may slip, I may even falter (we are all weak), but reach the top rung of the ladder I will!!! When there, my voice shall be heard, for I will shout to the multitudes below: 'Vici!' For the present I am only an amateur, and my work is unknown, forsooth, save to a party of friends, with here and there an enemy.

"But, Mr. Pooter, let me ask you, 'What is the difference between the amateur and the professional?'

"None!!!

"Stay! Yes, there is a difference. One is paid for doing what the other does as skilfully for nothing!

"But I will be paid, too! For I, contrary to the wishes of my family and friends, have at last elected to adopt the stage as my profession. And when the farce craze is over—and, mark you, that will be soon—I will make my power known; for I feel—pardon my apparent conceit—that there is no living man who can play the hump-backed Richard as I feel and know I can.

"And you will be the first to come round and bend your head in submission. There are many matters you may understand, but

knowledge of the fine art of acting is to you an unknown quantity.

"Pray let this discussion cease with this letter. Vale!

Yours truly,

"BURWIN-FOSSELTON."

Pa's response was outrage.

When Lupin came in, I handed him this impertinent letter, and said: "My boy, in that letter you can see the true character of your friend."

Lupin, to my surprise, said: "Oh yes. He showed me the letter before he sent it. I think he is right, and you ought to apologise."

That was daft of me – to provoke Pa. But sons do provoke fathers if they do not want to be supine replicas.

I suppose that the fact that I was doing well at work perked me up or gave me the confidence to say what I did. Pa did not apologise, of course.

There is now another strange gap in Pa's diary as it does not resume for nearly three weeks.

During those three weeks, I found myself missing Daisy.

"Dumped you has she," Sarah whispered one evening in the kitchen.

"How is your Mr Peters?"

"Kind, loving – and mine. And don't start eating before dinner. If you get fat, no girl will look at you," she said as she flounced away.

But if you're not getting any kissing, you want something else between your lips. I made myself two slices of bread, butter and jam. Sarah saw me as I came out of the kitchen.

"You've got strawberry jam round your lips. Very attractive," she sniped.

So both Pa and Sarah were getting at me. All I needed after my rupture with Daisy. Pa's next entry shows again his understandable wish to be seen as someone of a better class. He had not been to Oxford University. I don't think he'd even been to Oxford station yet he noted:

December 17.—As I open my scribbling diary I find the words "Oxford Michaelmas Term ends." Why this should induce me to indulge in retrospective I don't know, but it does. The last few weeks of my diary are of minimum interest. The breaking off of the engagement between Lupin and Daisy Mutlar has made him a different being, and Carrie a rather depressing companion. She was a little dull last Saturday, and I thought to cheer her up by reading some extracts from my diary; but she walked out of the room in the middle of the reading, without a word. On her return, I said: "Did my diary bore you, darling?"

She replied, to my surprise: "I really wasn't listening, dear. I was obliged to leave to give instructions to the laundress. In consequence of some stuff she puts in the water, two more of Lupin's coloured shirts have run and he says he won't wear them."

I said: "Everything is Lupin. It's all Lupin, Lupin, Lupin. There was not a single button on my shirt yesterday, but I made no complaint."

The pathetic plea of the jealous Pa. This is the heart of the modern discoveries of psychologists – the rivalry of fathers and sons. I have now read Freud's *Totem and Taboo*, where he explains this rivalry is as old as humanity. It has been festering since our ancestors covered themselves in woad and spent their days hunting woolly mammoths. They didn't realise how lucky they were, I say. Neanderthal man was not cooped up in dingy offices having to write up ledgers for Stone Age Perkupps so they could pay local butchers for a pound of mammoth mince. They could roam the jungles, eat berries and gaze at the stars un-obscured by pea soupers. Could be in B.C. that they even discussed their personal relationships because civilisation had not repressed them.

Stone Age father and son talk went like this, if one is to believe the psychologists. I like to picture them in their loin clothes squabbling over mammoth leftovers.

"Why are you staring at me like that Pa," son would say irritably.

"I am going to die before you so I hate you, boy, and want to kill you."

"That's quite understandable, Pa."

"No it isn't. Dads are not allowed to slaughter their sons."

"Apart from Abraham who the Lord told to take Isaac to the top of the mountain and then sacrifice him with sweet smelling spices."

"I'm glad you learned your Bible, son."

"What I want to do isn't even mentioned in the Bible, Pa."

"Let me guess. Drive a locomotive."

"I gave that up when I was three."

"Cocky aren't you? Something worse. Fly up in a balloon and piss over London."

"Get your head out of the clouds, Pa."

"Don't be cheeky, boy." At which point Neanderthal Pa cuffed Neanderthal son round the lug hole.

"If you want to know, I really want to sleep with Ma."

"Disgusting."

"The unconscious is disgusting, Pa."

"And ridiculous as you are only four, son."

"And much smaller than you, Pa, and I'd have to kill you in order to get my way."

"Your mother's been wanting to kill me for years so she'd be pleased."

"Typical, Pa. When you face something difficult, you make a joke out of it."

I can't blame Pa for not being aware of the contortions of the unconscious. In 1893, Sigmund Freud hadn't even begun to analyse his own dreams.

I have also now discovered Freud was a natty dresser. When he had enough clients on his couch, he ordered a new suit every six months. I don't know what Mrs Freud thought about that but my mother would have approved. There were often tensions between Ma and Pa concerning his dress, as he recorded that evening.

Carrie simply replied: "You should do as all other men do, and wear studs. In fact, I never saw anyone but you wear buttons on the shirt-fronts."

I said: "I certainly wore none yesterday, for there were none on."

Another thought that strikes me is that Gowing seldom calls in the evening, and Cummings never does. I fear they don't get on well with Lupin.

This is total nonsense. Gowing and Cummings saw me as

a promising young man and were glad, as they liked larks, that I added something to the gaiety of our street, Brickfield Terrace. But it was hard for Pa to see my gaiety – and probably he was a bit of a muffin because he had been snubbed by Daisy. Just like I had been.

December 18.—Yesterday I was in a retrospective vein—today it is prospective. I see nothing but clouds, clouds, clouds. Lupin is perfectly intolerable over the Daisy Mutlar business. He won't say what is the cause of the breach. He is evidently condemning her conduct, and yet, if we venture to agree with him, says he won't hear a word against her. So what is one to do? Another thing which is disappointing to me is, that Carrie and Lupin take no interest whatever in my diary.

I broached the subject at the breakfast-table to-day. I said: "I was in hopes that, if anything ever happened to me, the diary would be an endless source of pleasure to you both; to say nothing of the chance of the remuneration which may accrue from its being published."

Both Carrie and Lupin burst out laughing. Carrie was sorry for this, I could see, for she said: "I did not mean to be rude, dear Charlie; but truly I do not think your diary would sufficiently interest the public to be taken up by a publisher."

I replied: "I am sure it would prove quite as interesting as some of the ridiculous reminiscences that have been published lately. Besides, it's the diary that makes the man. Where would Evelyn and Pepys have been if it had not been for their diaries?"

Carrie said I was quite a philosopher:

Samuel Pepys

Poor Pa to compare himself to such giants. It was not Pepys' diary that made Charles II appoint him to help run the Navy. John Evelyn was not middling clerk, but born with a silver spoon in his mouth which turned to copper. Evelyn's son, John married Anne, whose father, Edward Boscawen of Cornwall, had legendary copper mines, which made him rich. They produced over 100,000 tons of copper ore, and 27,000 tons of arsenic. Brickfield Terrace didn't produce anything but hot air!

I gently told Pa that I didn't think his diary would be as interesting or as stylish as Pepys' or Evelyn's.

Lupin, in a jeering tone, said: "If it had been written on larger paper, Guv., we might get a fair price from a butterman for it."

As I am in the prospective vein, I vow the end of this year will see the end of my diary.

I was a bit sharp and I wished I hadn't said it.

December 19.—

We were coming up to Christmas, the holiday when families get together, but for us Pooters, that was not so simple given the secrets both my parents protected.

By 1893 Ma's mother was in her 60s. She was still in service making her pies, but Pa had no idea she was alive. Ma did visit her three or four times a year secretly as I said earlier, but she now could not pretend she was delivering laundry. So she told Pa she was going to see Mrs James of the séances. Mrs James knew Ma 'used' her in this way, which is why she felt free to behave in such a domineering manner when she came to stay with us.

Pa himself could not admit his own truth. His father was dead and he had no idea where he was buried. He also had no where his mother lived or if she was even alive. So the invitation in his diary is a complete fantasy. But I didn't know that when I played the radical know it all.

The annual invitation came to spend Christmas with Carrie's mother—the usual family festive gathering to which we always look forward. Lupin declined to go. I was astounded, and expressed my surprise and disgust. Lupin then obliged us with the following Radical speech: "I hate a family gathering at Christmas. What does it mean? Why someone says: 'Ah! we miss poor Uncle James, who was here last year,' and we all begin to snivel. Someone else says: 'It's two years since poor Aunt Liz used to sit in that corner.' Then we all begin to snivel again. Then another gloomy relation says 'Ah! I wonder whose turn it will be next.' Then we all snivel again, and proceed to eat and drink too much; and they don't discover until I get up that we have been seated thirteen at dinner."

December 20 – Pa spent the whole evening talking to Ma about who to send cards to. Mr Perkupp got the most fancy and most expensive one. Gowing and Cummings got second best. Pa also sent cards to customers that he had dealings with, adding that he had been honoured to work on their accounts. Ma insisted that Mrs James should get one as magnificent as Perkupp's. By the end of the evening they had written 24 cards. I had to decide whether or not to send

Pa, Gowing and Cummings – and me behind

Daisy one. In the end I found a saucy card for my once beloved who didn't fancy kissing.

December 21.—To save the postman a miserable Christmas, we follow the example of all unselfish people, and send out our cards early. Most of the cards had finger-marks, which I did not notice at night. I shall buy all future cards in the daytime. Lupin (who, ever since he has had the appointment with a stock and share broker, does not seem over-scrupulous in his dealings) told me never to rub out the pencilled price on the backs of the cards. I asked him why. Lupin said: "Suppose your card is marked 9d. Well, all you have to do is to pencil a 3—and a long down-stroke after it—in front of the nine pence, and people will think you have given five times the price for it."

Pa makes me out to be a forger and a cheapskate, which was not very paternal of Pa. But given what I have said about conflict between fathers and sons, I could hardly be surprised.

In the evening Lupin was very low-spirited, and I reminded him that behind the clouds the sun was shining. He said: "Ugh! it never shines on me." I said: "Stop, Lupin, my boy; you are worried about Daisy Mutlar. Don't think of her any more. You ought to congratulate yourself on having got off a very bad bargain. Her notions are far too grand for our simple tastes." He jumped up and said: "I won't allow one word to be uttered against her. She's worth the whole bunch of your friends put together, that inflated, sloping-head of a Perkupp included."

I had finally said what I thought of Perkupp. Pa looked

shocked beyond measure and it affected his sense of balance. He wrote:

I left the room with silent dignity, but caught my foot in the mat.

That was just the kind of accident which made Freud's marbles thrill. Pa's unconscious tripped him up because his conscious mind could not allow him to hear, let alone, utter any anti-Perkuppness. As Marx said, the bosses don't just steal all your bananas, but twist their way into your soul – till it isn't your own.

December 23.—I exchanged no words with Lupin in the morning; but as he seemed to be in exuberant spirits in the evening, I ventured to ask him where he intended to spend his Christmas. He replied: "Oh, most likely at the Mutlars'."

In wonderment, I said: "What! after your engagement has been broken off?"

Lupin said: "Who said it is off?"

I said: "You have given us both to understand—"

He interrupted me by saying: "Well, never mind what I said. It is on again—there!"

It was the Xmas card that did it. Daisy sent me word she wanted to meet me at the Oyster and Fiddle. I was there fifteen minutes ahead of the time she had suggested. She had done up her hair very carefully.

"I'm sorry," she said and took my hand.

"I did only try to kiss you."

Karl Marx, my intellectual inspiration

She blushed. "I better tell you something, dearest."

I squeezed her hand to encourage her to trust me.

"I worry about such things … they call them intimacies," Daisy whispered.

"Are you going to tell me why?"

"When we're married … but meanwhile…"

She laced her fingers in mine, and held my hand to her lips and kissed it.

When we finished our beers, we went outside. She put her arms round me and kissed me quite passionately.

"I've been practising," she said coming up for air, and added: "In the mirror, dumbkins. There'll be more when we're on honeymoon. Now let's do something I really like."

She raced inside and talked to the publican. Ten minutes later she was singing – beautifully I have to admit.

In his diary Pa continued to write as if they had been to see Ma's mother.

December 26.—I did not sleep very well last night; I never do in a strange bed. I feel a little indigestion, which one must expect at this time of the year. Carrie and I returned to Town in the evening. Lupin came in late. He said he enjoyed his Christmas, and added: "I feel as fit as a Lowther Arcade fiddle, and only require a little more 'oof' to feel as fit as a £500 Stradivarius." I have long since given up trying to understand Lupin's slang, or asking him to explain it.

Their Xmas trip was to Blackheath where they stayed in a bed and breakfast, Ma admitted to me years later. They walked through Greenwich Park and gazed out over the Thames and London. Pa liked to stand on the meridian so that he had one foot in the Eastern and one foot in the Western hemisphere. He'd have liked to put that in the diary but it would reveal they had no family to go to at Christmas. Children aren't supposed to lie to their parents but if parents lie to their kids, it seems acceptable. Pa's diary continued blithely:

December 27.—I told Lupin I was expecting Gowing and Cummings to drop in tomorrow evening for a quiet game. I was in hope the boy would volunteer to stay in, and help to amuse them. Instead of which, he said: "Oh, you had better put them off, as I have asked Daisy and Frank Mutlar to come." I said I could not think of doing such a thing. Lupin said: "Then I will send a wire, and put off Daisy." I suggested that a post-card or letter would reach her quite soon enough, and would not be so extravagant.

For once, she was on Pa's side, which upset me, of course.

Carrie, who had listened to the above conversation with apparent annoyance, directed a well-aimed shaft at Lupin. She said: "Lupin, why do you object to Daisy meeting your father's friends? Is it because they are not good enough for her, or (which is equally possible) she is not good enough for them?" Lupin was dumbfounded, and could make no reply. When he left the room, I gave Carrie a kiss of approval.

December 28—Lupin, on coming down to breakfast, said to his mother: "I have not put off Daisy and Frank, and should like them to join Gowing and Cummings this evening." I felt very pleased with the boy for this. Carrie said, in reply: "I am glad you let me know in time, as I can turn over the cold leg of mutton, dress it with a little parsley, and no one will know it has been cut." She further said she would make a few custards, and stew some pippins, so that they would be cold by the evening.

Finding Lupin in good spirits, I asked him quietly if he really had any personal objection to either Gowing or Cummings. He replied: "Not in the least. I think Cummings looks rather an ass, but that is partly due to his patronising 'the three-and-six-one-price hat company,' and wearing a reach-me-down frock-coat. As for that perpetual brown velveteen jacket of Gowing's—why, he resembles an itinerant photographer."

I said it was not the coat that made the gentleman; whereupon Lupin, with a laugh, replied: "No, and it wasn't much of a gentleman who made their coats."

That evening, Daisy was in a sweet mood when she came in. She put her arms round me. Sarah saw this, and the next I knew, she had knocked over a vase.

"You'll pay for that out of your wages," Pa shouted.

"It's the time of good cheer, Pa," Ma said. "It was just an accident."

"So sorry," Sarah said. "I'll mop it up." She rushed away and came back with a broom. I bent down and helped her. Daisy looked startled. I sensed Pa was about to protest it was Sarah's mess to clear up but Ma nudged him. He left the room and only came back when it was time to eat.

We were rather jolly at supper, and Daisy made herself very agreeable, especially in the earlier part of the evening, when she sang. At supper, however, she said: "Can you make tee-to-tums with bread?" and she commenced rolling up pieces of bread, and twisting them round on the table. I felt this to be bad manners, but of course said nothing. Presently Daisy and Lupin, to my disgust, began throwing bread-pills at each other. Frank followed suit, and so did Cummings and Gowing, to my astonishment.

They then commenced throwing hard pieces of crust, one piece catching me on the forehead, and making me blink. I said: "Steady, please; steady!" Frank jumped up and said: "Tum, tum; then the band played."

I can't let this description of throwing bread pills go without comment, as I have identified an influence Pa's diary had on literature which would have given him more than a crumb of comfort. Seriously he'd have been chuffed. I don't think that anyone before him had described a scene where the heroes pelted each other with bread. The literary importance is that it seems likely P.G Wodehouse got the idea for one of his recurring comic set pieces from Pa's diary. When the diary came out, Wodehouse was still a schoolboy and had not published one word. Wooster, Jeeves and the Drones Club weren't even in his dreams. At Jeeves' club for gentlemen's gentlemen, The Ganymede, bread pelting was never allowed, but once members of the Drones had been conjured up, they were always letting off steam. They did not have any experience of suffering in salt mines or our modern salt mines, offices in the City, so why did they have to let off? The self-indulgence of the bourgeoisie, Marx would have said.

Wodehouse himself was not born with a silver spoon in his mouth, and he had his own experiences of a kind of Perkupp.

Wodehouse could not afford to go to Oxford and spent part of his early career bent over the ledgers at The Hongkong and Shanghai Banking Corporation in Lombard Street. His financial career was short and far from glittering. In his first year he was late for work on 20 days (excluding 'foggy mornings', which did not count) – a number only exceeded by two of his 56 contemporaries! Readers will see similarities with myself.

Wodehouse later admitted in a memoir for the bank staff magazine that:

"If there was a moment in the course of my banking career

when I had the remotest notion of what it was all about, I am unable to recall it. From Fixed Deposits I drifted to Inward Bills – no use asking me what Inward Bills are, I never found out... My total inability to grasp what was going on made me something of a legend in the place."

He indulged in bankotage, sabotage perpetrated on banks, in case you have not worked it out.

Upon seeing the pristine new ledger before him, he could not resist the chance to write a comical piece on the front page. He thought better of it afterwards and cut out the page with his pen knife. The head cashier came across the damaged ledger some days later, and blamed the bank's stationers. The angry stationers argued that the page had been cut out. Wodehouse remembered the incident:

'Absurd', the head cashier replied, 'nobody but an imbecile would cut out the first page of a ledger'.

Here Wodehouse met his Perkupp for the unnamed senior replied: 'Then you must have an imbecile in your department. Have you?'

'Why, yes', the cashier admitted, for he was a fair-minded man. 'There is P.G Wodehouse.' They got me under the lights and grilled me, and I had to come clean, Wodehouse confessed.

Like I had done in Oldham, Wodehouse realised his days at the bank were numbered. So he started to write short stories, articles, lyrics, poems and jokes for dozens of magazines. 1902, he left the ledgers to become a full-time writer.

Wodehouse immortalised his time in the Square Mile in Psmith in the City. The Hong Kong and Shanghai Bank becomes the New Asiatic Bank, where Psmith is a reluctant banker. Reluctance was hardly strange, as when the book came out in 1910, clerks were still adding up in copperplate. They often were not allowed to use the adding machines that were then available.

I said Pa had his moments. Wodehouse never acknowledged the diary had been his inspiration. For all my problems with Pa, I want him to have his niche in literary history. Our conflicts were not that unusual and I recall the times of bread battles with some affection. Pa went on:

I did not know what this meant, but they all roared, and continued the bread-battle. Gowing suddenly seized all the parsley off the cold mutton, and threw it full in my face. I looked daggers at Gowing, who replied: "I say, it's no good trying to look indignant, with your hair full of parsley." I rose from the table, and insisted that a stop should be put to this foolery at once. Frank Mutlar shouted: "Time, gentlemen, please! time!" and turned out the gas, leaving us in absolute darkness.

I was feeling my way out of the room, when I suddenly received a hard intentional punch at the back of my head. I said loudly: "Who did that?" There was no answer; so I repeated the question, with the same result. I struck a match, and lighted the gas. They were all talking and laughing, so I kept my own counsel; but, after they had gone, I said to Carrie: "The person who sent me that insulting post-card at Christmas was here to-night."

I am glad that Pa never found out I threw the punch; there are things it's best fathers never find out. Feeling my frustration, I decided to make myself scarce the next day.

December 30, Sunday.—Lupin spent the whole day with the Mutlars. He seemed rather cheerful in the evening, so I said: "I'm glad to see you so happy, Lupin." He answered: "Well, Daisy is a splendid girl, but I was obliged to take her old fool of a father down a peg. What with his meanness over his cigars, his stinginess over his drinks, his farthing economy in turning down the gas if you only quit the room for a second, writing to one on half-sheets of note-paper, sticking the remnant of the last cake of soap on to the new cake, putting two bricks on each side of the fireplace, and his general 'outside-halfpenny-'bus-ness,' I was compelled to let him have a bit of my mind." I said: "Lupin, you are not much more than a boy; I hope you won't repent it."

Fathers are a fraternity. They sense that the young have it in for them, so it was no surprise Pa sided with Mutthead Mutlar. What I didn't expect was that Mutlar would try to cajole Pa on to his side.

December 31.—The last day of the Old Year. I received an extraordinary letter from Mr. Mutlar, senior. He writes: "Dear Sir,—For a long time past I have had considerable difficulty deciding the important question, 'Who is the master of my own house? Myself, or your son Lupin?' Believe me, I have no prejudice one way or the other; but I have been most reluctantly compelled to give judgment to the effect that I am the master of it. Under the circumstances, it has become my duty to forbid your son to enter my house again. I am sorry, because it deprives me of the society of one of the most modest, unassuming, and gentlemanly persons I have ever had the honour of being acquainted with."

I did not desire the last day to wind up disagreeably, so I said nothing to either Carrie or Lupin about the letter.

A most terrible fog came on, and Lupin would go out in it, but promised to be back to drink out the Old Year—a custom we have always observed.

At a quarter to twelve Lupin had not returned, and the fog was fearful. As time was drawing close, I got out the spirits. Carrie and I deciding on whisky, I opened a fresh bottle; but Carrie said it smelt like brandy. As I knew it to be whisky, I said there was nothing to discuss. Carrie, evidently vexed that Lupin had not come in, did discuss it all the same, and wanted me to have a small wager with her to decide by the smell. I said I could decide it by the taste in a moment. A silly and unnecessary argument followed, the result of which was we suddenly saw it was a quarter-past twelve, and, for the first time in our married life, we missed welcoming in the New Year. Lupin got home at a quarter-past two, having got lost in the fog—so he said.

I wasn't lost but upset. I had gone out, but as luck would have it, Sarah and her ageing beau, the faithful besotted Peters, were drinking champagne in the pub that I walked to. I didn't want to talk to them so I waved cheerily at her and left. I got home later as Pa wrote, and was just getting into my pyjamas when Sarah walked into my room – without knocking.

I quickly draped my blanket round me.

"I came to wish the man who jilted me a Happy New Year."

"Happy New Year to you too," I replied frostily.

"It will be now I'm engaged to Mr Peters who isn't engaged to anyone else and only has eyes for me."

She sat down on the bed as she said it.

"Don't get any ideas," she whispered.

"We're both engaged to other people, it would be very improper," I said," to have any ideas."

"You only ever have one idea anyway."

"That's quite unfair."

"I bet your fiancé hasn't done this to you," Sarah said.

But she only did it for a minute.

"After all, you belong to Daisy," she smiled as she stopped, leaving me over excited, which was precisely what she wanted.

"And you belong to Mr Peters," I said as calmly as I could.

"I just belong to myself, Lupin," she replied. "That was just a New Year's gift. You won't get it ever again from me," she added, tip toeing out of my room.

I began to wonder if I had made a huge mistake in being engaged to Daisy who was worried about intimacies messing her hair-do.

I spent January 1 and 2 reading the financial papers, which were full of predictions for the coming year. Some said the market was too high; some said the market was too low. You could easily get very confused, something Pa found hard to handle.

January 3.—Still in a state of anxiety and excitement, which was not alleviated by ascertaining that Mr. Perkupp sent word he should not be at the office to-day. In the evening, Lupin, who was busily engaged with a paper, said suddenly to me: "Do you know anything about chalk pits, Guv.?" I said: "No, my boy, not that I'm aware of." Lupin said: "Well, I give you the tip; chalk pits are as safe as Consols, and pay six per cent. at par." I said a rather neat thing, viz.: "They may be six per cent. at par, but your pa has no money to invest." Carrie and I both roared with laughter. Lupin did not take the slightest notice of the joke, although I purposely repeated it for him; but continued: "I give you the tip, that's all—chalk pits!" I said another funny thing: "Mind you don't fall into them!" Lupin put on a supercilious smile, and said: "Bravo! Joe Miller."

Pa's one pun after another had left me exasperated which is why I dredge up Joe Miller (1684-1738). He wrote *An Immense Collection of the Funniest Jokes, Quaint and Laughable Anecdotes, Mirth Provoking Stories, Brilliant Witticisms, and Queer Sayings.* It was a very long title and had a very long life. It was republished many times between 1740 and 1890. Some say every joke you've ever heard is a variation on a joke in Miller's Jest Book. About half of the jokes are funny today and may still be funny in another 200 years or more. Thinking of how long things last, I wonder whether in two centuries, City slaves will still be divided into ranks as they were in Perkupp's dusty firm. Each rank had different pens which cost different amounts though in a surge towards rampant equality, they had all had identical inkwells.

The ranks there were:

Too young to be a clerk
Apprentice clerk
Junior Clerk
General Clerk
Senior Clerk
Too old to be a clerk

JOE
MILLER'S
Joke
Book
THE GREATEST OF JESTERS PRESENTS
JOKES, PUNS, GAGS, & QUIPS!

Pa was a general clerk and his ambition was to get promotion, but there were only two positions as senior clerk; neither man was near the age where they might retire.

In the diary Pa does not explain fully why he was suddenly in clerk heaven, that cloud where angels have inkwells and cherubim rub their noses in ledgers.

January 4.—Mr. Perkupp sent for me and told me that my position would be that of one of the senior clerks. I was more than overjoyed. Mr. Perkupp added, he would let me know tomorrow what the salary would be. This means another day's anxiety; I don't mind, for it is anxiety of the right sort.

One of the senior clerks, Mr Wordsworth, had begun to tremble, so his copper plate was more like copper wobble. Perkupp could not tolerate that; so the man was told to work only in the afternoons. Perkupp made much of the fact he did not dismiss him but kept him on at half pay at the rank of too old to be a clerk. Pa continued:

That reminded me that I had forgotten to speak to Lupin about the letter I received from Mr. Mutlar, senr. I broached the subject to Lupin in the evening, having first consulted Carrie. Lupin was riveted to the Financial News, as if he had been a born capitalist, and I said: "Pardon me a moment, Lupin, how is it you have not been to the Mutlars' any day this week?"

Lupin answered: "I told you! I cannot stand old Mutlar."

I said: "Mr. Mutlar writes to me to say pretty plainly that he cannot stand you!"

Lupin said: "Well, I like his cheek in writing to you. I'll find out if his father is still alive, and I will write him a note complaining of his son, and I'll state pretty clearly that his son is a blithering idiot!"

I said: "Lupin, please moderate your expressions in the presence of your mother."

Is 'blithering' an indecent word? No but my blithering father declared it to be when I used it.

Lupin said: "I'm very sorry, but there is no other expression one can apply to him. However, I'm determined not to enter his place again."

I said: "You know, Lupin, he has forbidden you the house."

Lupin replied: "Well, we won't split straws—it's all the same. Daisy is a trump, and will wait for me ten years, if necessary."

Was Daisy a trump, a tramp or a vamp? I did sometimes wonder in the privacy of my bedroom if her high and haughty might not be the ideal woman for me. About her father there was no doubt. The prospect of having Mutthead Mutlar as a father-in-law filled me with gloom. But the next day I forgot all my troubles.

I have said I loved Pa and so was delighted by what then was given to him.

January 5.—I can scarcely write the news. Mr. Perkupp told me my salary would be raised £100! I stood gaping for a moment unable to realise it. I annually get £10 rise, and I thought it might be £15 or even £20; but £100 surpasses all belief. Carrie and I both rejoiced over our good fortune. Lupin came home in the evening in the utmost good spirits. I sent Sarah quietly round to the grocer's for a bottle of champagne, the same as we had before, "Jackson Frères." It was opened at supper, and I said to Lupin: "This is to celebrate some good news I have received to-day." Lupin replied: "Hooray, Guv.! And I have some good news, also; a double event, eh?" I said: "My boy, as a result of twenty-one years' industry and strict attention to the interests of my superiors in office, I have been rewarded with promotion and a rise in salary of £100."

Lupin gave three cheers, and we rapped the table furiously, which brought in Sarah to see what the matter was. Lupin ordered us to "fill up" again, and addressing us upstanding, said: "Having been in the firm of Job Cleanands, stock and share-brokers, a few weeks, and not having paid particular attention to the interests of my superiors in office, my Guv'nor, as a reward to me, allotted me £5 worth of shares in a really good thing. The result is, to-day I have made £200." I said: "Lupin, you are joking." "No, Guv., it's the good old truth; Job Cleanands put me on to Chlorates."

No event in this book shows better the rivalries between fathers and sons. Pa had just had a triumph. His son, me, could not let him enjoy it in peace. I had to trump his success with my success. I had to have a bigger chunk of mammoth; my cucumber had to out-cumber Pa's. I wish I had not been unkind and let him revel in his well-deserved salary rise.

I was on a swagger with my £200, and decided to offer myself the kind of experience rich young bucks had. First I bought a new suit and a cravat at a smart tailor's in Savile Row. Then I hailed a hansom. Hansom drivers knew all the places men were not supposed to visit but did all the same.

Madame Romanova's Palace of Russian Beauties was a magnificent house in Chelsea. Two footmen dressed as Cossacks stood outside. There were flaming torches by the entrance. Getting inside required cosying up to the Cossacks.

"What is your name," the taller Cossack smiled.

I felt the devil on my lips so I gave my name as "Perkupp."

"How do you know of our palace?"

"It's famous in society," I smiled.

"Did someone recommend you?"

I was conscious that my unconscious was so anxious I almost wanted the Cossacks to send me away, so I gave them the name of a greatest pleasure seeker of our time.

"The Prince of Wales. His Highness said there were no Russian beauties as beautiful as those who grace your palace."

"Welcome," they opened the door for me.

I walked into an opulent living room which was unusual in two ways. There were ten sofas and on eight them, young women were sitting almost like mannequins. In the middle, a violinist was playing with great energy. From time to time, he gave one of the girls his bow and she spanked him with it. He yelped with exaggerated pain.

You could not imagine anything less like Caldwell's tatty dance hall but I knew you would not get in – or out – of here for a shilling or so.

"What is your name," Madame Romanova shook my hand. She was an elegant lady well past middle age.

"Perkupp," I said.

"I think one of your uncles has occasionally visited us."

I was startled. Could it be that Perkupp had a secret life with secret lusts?

"He said that here nightly it was sprightly," I smiled.

"You are a poet," Madame said. "Normally we ask new visitors to make a contribution before we discuss what entertainment they'd like but as we know your uncle, we will let that pass."

"Most kind, Madame."

"Now you must have some vodka."

A waiter, also dressed as a Cossack, appeared with a tall glass.

"We call this cocktail a black Russian though we have only white Russians here. We can obtain black Russians, of course, if desired." And if the customer could pay for such exotic girls.

I sipped the cocktail and, while I was doing that, one of the reclining blondes came up to me.

"This is Ludmila. She comes from Siberia which is very cold but she is very warm," Madame smiled.

Ludmila took my arm.

"Let me warm you up upstairs," she said. She sounded more cockney than Russian though. She led me to a beautiful room which had mirrors on every wall.

She closed the door. "Are you a voyeur, duckie," she asked.

"Is duckie a Russian word?"

"Yes, it means lollipop, darling. I don't think you know what a voyeur is."

"And I think you're more likely to come from Poplar than Moscow," I said.

One of the photographs on the walls of the Russian Palace. The bicycle makes me think she came from Birmingham.

"Do you really care? "

"No."

"Why don't you let me make you comfortable?" Ludmila took my jacket off me and undid my cravat. She folded the clothes carefully and put them on a chair.

"So Ludmila introduced you to the passions of the Russians," Madame said when I came down an hour later. "We have many other girls who would like to perkupp with you. Or you could stay the whole night. "

"I must go, sadly."

Of course I couldn't go before I handed over ten pounds for destitute Russian orphans.

I thought I had got rather more for two pounds with Rosie in the days of my innocence in Oldham.

So the next Saturday, I told Ma I had to go and meet someone in the way of business when in fact I took the Great Northern back to Oldham.

I wasn't surprised to find Rosie in our old pub, but I was very surprised by the company she was keeping.

"Where have you been," she smiled when she saw me.

"In London."

"I'm engaged now," Rosie smiled.

"So am I. Probably."

"How can you be engaged probably. I'm engaged definitely," she said.

"Where is the lucky man?"

"He's powdering his peg," she laughed. "But I can't say that kind of thing to him. He's a real gentleman."

I was surprised to see Mr Down at the bar and then even more surprised when he brought a port and lemon for Rosie.

"This is Albert," she said.

Rosie had got engaged to Mr Down. He was not happy to see me.

"If you bother my fiancé again I'll whip you," Down snarled. "This idiot once turned up at the bank wearing a dog muzzle."

"Keep your hair on Albie," Rosie said, which I thought Down would find hard as he was bald. I stared and realised with some shock that Down was no longer bald.

"Lupin was once in love with me. He can't help it."

"He is a young hound," Down said.

"And you're a bit of an old hound," Rosie said," but I like 'em mature."

Down wasn't pleased to be called mature.

"Like a blue cheese," I smiled and then I spotted it. "You're wearing a wig," I pointed out.

"You haven't changed one bit," he snarled.

I had learned a few tricks with the Holloway Comedians. Deftly, I managed to remove Down's wig which he hadn't stuck on very securely.

"You need to get better glue," I said. And tossed the wig to the barman who caught it.

"It smells vile," the barman said as he dunked it in a barrel of stout. Down retrieved it and tried to shake it dry.

Rosie couldn't stop laughing.

"I'll let you have your fun in peace, Mr Down. But I thought you should know I now work at £200 a year for Cleanands."

"How much," Rosie said with sudden interest.

"He's lying like he always did," Down said, trying to fit his wig back on. By now the whole pub was screeching with laughter.

It was a mistake trying to re visit old haunts but I didn't want to say that as it might upset Rosie. "Good luck Rosie," I said.

"Good luck Lupin," she got up and hugged me.

As I walked away, I heard her say to Down: "You better earn more than he does. I didn't know you had less hair than streaky bacon."

So I went back to London having learned something … never go back.

With my new salary I decided I could afford a little luxury which of course Pa disapproved of.

January 21.—I am very much concerned at Lupin having started a pony-trap. I said: "Lupin, are you justified in this outrageous extravagance?" Lupin replied: "Well, one must get to the City somehow. I've only hired it, and can give it up any time I like." I repeated my question: "Are you justified in this extravagance?" He replied: "Look here, Guv., excuse me saying so, but you're a bit out of date. It does not pay nowadays, fiddling about over small things. I don't mean anything personal, Guv'nor. My boss says if I take his tip, and stick to big things, I can make big money!" I said I thought the very idea of speculation most horrifying. Lupin said "It is not speculation, it's a dead cert." I advised him, at all events, not to continue the pony and cart; but he replied: "I made £200 in one day; now suppose I only make £200 in a month, or put it at £100 a month, which is ridiculously low—why, that is £1,250 a year. What's a few pounds a week for a trap?"

Till I was 21, Pa was still responsible for my debts and he worried I'd end up ruining him. He dreaded ruin, being the son of a ruined man and a ruined woman. But he never even hinted at that past.

I did not pursue the subject further, beyond saying that I should feel glad when the autumn came, and Lupin would be of age and responsible for his own debts. He answered: "My dear

Guv, I promise you faithfully that I will never speculate with what I have not got. I shall only go on Job Cleanands' tips, and as he is in the 'know' it is pretty safe sailing." I felt somewhat relieved. Gowing called in the evening and, to my surprise, informed me that, as he had made £10 by one of Lupin's tips, he intended asking us and the Cummings round next Saturday. Carrie and I said we should be delighted.

For once I had done something Pa approved of, but his approval didn't last long.

February 10, Sunday.—Contrary to my wishes, Carrie allowed Lupin to persuade her to take her for a drive in the afternoon in his trap. I quite disapprove of driving on a Sunday, but I did not like to trust Carrie alone with Lupin, so I offered to go too. Lupin said: "Now, that is nice of you, Guv, but you won't mind sitting on the back-seat of the cart?"

Lupin proceeded to put on a bright-blue coat that seemed miles too large for him. Carrie said it wanted taking in considerably at the back. Lupin said: "Haven't you seen a box-coat before? You can't drive in anything else."

He may wear what he likes in the future, for I shall never drive with him again. His conduct was shocking. When we passed Highgate Archway, he tried to pass everything and everybody. He shouted to respectable people who were walking quietly in the road to get out of the way; he flicked at the horse of an old man who was riding, causing it to rear; and, as I had to ride backwards, I was compelled to face a gang of roughs in a donkey-cart, whom Lupin had chaffed, and who turned and followed us for nearly a mile, bellowing, indulging in coarse jokes and laughter, to say nothing of occasionally pelting us with orange-peel.

Pa did get things out of proportion. In 1889, Jack the Ripper terrified London but his atrocious crimes were part of the fabric of a city where violence was everyday. The fight in the pub, the stab in the dark, the husband hitting his wife, bitterness, drink, swagger. My shouting from the trap was small beer. I said something of the sort to Pa, dragging in the royal who had recommended Madame Romanova's to me.

Lupin's excuse—that the Prince of Wales would have to put up with the same sort of thing if he drove to the Derby—was of little consolation to either Carrie or myself. Frank Mutlar called in the evening, and Lupin went out with him.

February 11.—Feeling a little concerned about Lupin, I mustered up courage to speak to Mr. Perkupp about him. Mr. Perkupp has always been most kind to me, so I told him everything, including yesterday's adventure. Mr. Perkupp kindly replied: "There is no necessity for you to be anxious, Mr. Pooter. It would be impossible for a son of such good parents to turn out erroneously. Remember he is young, and will soon get older. I wish we could find room for him in this firm." The advice of this good man takes loads off my mind.

When I read this I felt sick because the idea of slaving for 'good man' Perkupp horrified me. He'd probably make me carry a ledger on my head and recite "Perkupp is the best of men." I went out for a long walk. I wondered if perhaps I didn't owe it to Pa to do something that would please him. I came back in time to eat and after we finished, I cleared my throat.

After our little supper, Lupin said: "My dear parents, I have some news, which I fear will affect you considerably." I felt a qualm come over me, and said nothing. Lupin then said: "It may distress you—in fact, I'm sure it will—but this afternoon I have given up my pony and trap for ever." It may seem absurd, but I was so pleased, I immediately opened a bottle of port.

So Pa was pleased. He added:

Gowing dropped in just in time, bringing with him a large sheet, with a print of a tailless donkey, which he fastened against the wall. He then produced several separate tails, and we spent the remainder of the evening trying blindfolded to pin a tail on in the proper place. My sides positively ached with laughter when I went to bed.

By the time Gowing left we were all tired. I went to my room, half hoping Sarah would knock on the door, but she didn't.

February 12.—In the evening I spoke to Lupin about his engagement with Daisy Mutlar. I asked if he had heard from her. He replied: "No; she promised that old windbag of a father of hers that she would not communicate with me. I see Frank Mutlar, of course; in fact, he said he might call again this evening." Frank called, but said he could not stop, as he had a friend waiting outside for him, named Murray Posh, adding he was quite a swell. Carrie asked Frank to bring him in.

He was brought in, Gowing entering at the same time. Mr. Murray Posh was a tall, fat young man, and was evidently of a very nervous disposition, as he subsequently confessed he would never go in a hansom cab, nor would he enter a four-wheeler until the driver had first got on the box with his reins in his hands.

On being introduced, Gowing, with his usual want of tact, said: "Any relation to 'Posh's three-shilling hats'?" Mr. Posh replied: "Yes; but please understand I don't try on hats myself. I take no active part in the business." I replied: "I wish I had a business like it." Mr. Posh seemed pleased, and gave a long but most interesting history of the extraordinary difficulties in the manufacture of cheap hats.

Again let me put this context. In 1893, the hat was a mark of class and the top hat was top class. The topper got its big break in 1853 when Prince Albert started wearing one. Royals always set fashion and what the Prince wore, the whole country soon wanted to wear.

Pa concentrated rather on the relationship between Posh and Daisy:

Murray Posh evidently knew Daisy Mutlar very intimately from the way he was talking of her; and Frank said to Lupin once, laughingly: "If you don't look out, Posh will cut you out!" When they had all gone, I referred to this flippant conversation; and Lupin said, sarcastically: "A man who is jealous has no respect for himself. A man who would be jealous of an elephant like Murray Posh could only have contempt for himself. I know Daisy. She would wait ten years for me, as I said before; in fact, if necessary, she would wait twenty years for me."

Carrie said: "Mark my words, Charles, some misfortune is about to happen."

I said: "Nonsense, dear."

In the evening Lupin arrived home early, and seemed a little agitated. I said: "What's up, my boy?" He hesitated a good deal, and then said: "You know those Parachikka Chlorates I advised you to invest £20 in?" I replied: "Yes, they are all right, I trust?" He replied: "Well, no! To the surprise of everybody, they have utterly collapsed."

My breath was so completely taken away, I could say nothing. Carrie looked at me, and said: "What did I tell you?" Lupin, after a while, said: "However, you are specially fortunate. I received an early tip, and sold out yours immediately, and was fortunate to get £2 for them. So you get something after all."

I gave a sigh of relief. I said: "I was not so sanguine as to suppose, as you predicted, that I should get six or eight times the amount of my investment; still a profit of £2 is a good percentage for such a short time." Lupin said, quite irritably: "You don't understand. I sold your £20 shares for £2; you therefore lose £18 on the transaction, whereby Cummings and Gowing will lose the whole of theirs."

I anticipated a furious reaction. Instead, I got a lecture and I promised to repay his losses as soon as I could.

"That's very decent of you, Lupin," Pa said, but he couldn't resist adding: "If you ever get a decent berth."

February 19.—Lupin, before going to town, said: "I am very sorry about those Parachikka Chlorates; it would not have happened if the boss, Job Cleanands, had been in town. Between ourselves, you must not be surprised if something goes wrong at our office. Job Cleanands has not been seen the last few days, and it strikes me several people do want to see him very particularly."

In the evening Lupin was just on the point of going out to avoid a collision with Gowing and Cummings, when the former entered the room, without knocking, but with his usual trick of saying, "May I come in?"

I had begun to wonder about Job Cleanands's disappearance, and if he had decided to flee, because his firm was in financial trouble like much of the Stock Market.

Argentina was the origin of the panic of 1893. The wheat crop failed and a military coup followed. European investors started a run on gold in the U.S. Treasury, since you could cash in dollar investments for exportable gold.

On February 20, 1893, thirteen days before the new American president Grover Cleveland, took office a major railway went bust. Cleveland convinced Congress to repeal the Sherman Silver Purchase Act, which he felt was mainly responsible for the crisis. Politicians usually can't work magic on a sick economy. Cleveland fit that bill. Despite his efforts, 15,000 companies and 500 banks failed. A fifth of American workers lost their jobs. A once-secure middle-class could not pay its mortgages. Many walked away from recently built homes before the banks sent the receivers in. No one had seen a crash like this before.

If there had been shares in soup kitchens, they would have

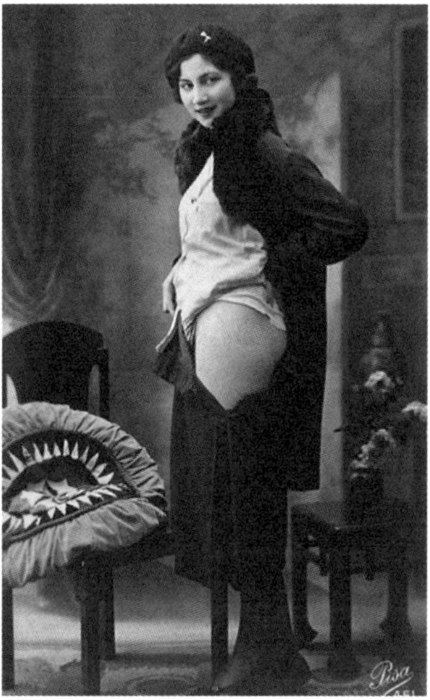

One of the other Russian beauties who came from Poplar and was popular

boomed. They opened in every city; hungry people chopped wood, broke rocks, and sewed for food. In some cases, women resorted to prostitution to feed their families.

In the end Cleveland had to borrow $65 million in gold from J.P. Morgan and the Rothschilds to support the gold standard. In the past, banks bailed out governments. Now governments were bailing out banks.

The panic even inspired a musical which ironically made money for its producers.

The panic also meant that City-slaves like Pa had to be even more humble and please Perkupp every moment.

At *The Laurels*, Gowing often came in without knocking. I wanted to avoid meeting him, but Gowing grabbed some cake and did not seem at all put on by his loss. Pa noted:

Gowing, to the surprise of Lupin and myself, seemed to be in the very best of spirits. Neither Lupin nor I broached the subject to him, but he did so of his own accord. He said: "I say, those Parachikka Chlorates have gone an awful smash! You're a nice one, Master Lupin. How much do you lose?" Lupin, to my utter astonishment, said: "Oh! I had nothing in them. There was some informality in my application—I forgot to enclose the cheque or something, and I didn't get any. The Guv loses £18." I said: "I quite understood you were in it, or nothing would have induced me to speculate." Lupin replied: "Well, it can't be helped; you must go double on the next tip." Before I could reply, Gowing said: "Well, I lose nothing, fortunately. From what I heard, I did not quite believe in them, so I persuaded Cummings to take my £15 worth, as he had more faith in them than I had."

Lupin burst out laughing, and, in the most unseemly manner, said: "Alas, poor Cummings. He'll lose £35." At that moment there was a ring at the bell. Lupin said: "I don't want to meet Cummings." If he had gone out of the door he would have met him in the passage, so as quickly as possible Lupin opened the parlour window and got out. Gowing jumped up suddenly, exclaiming: "I don't want to see him either!" and, before I could say a word, he followed Lupin out of the window.

For my own part, I was horrified to think my own son and one of my most intimate friends should depart from the house like a couple of interrupted burglars. Poor Cummings was very upset, and of course was naturally very angry both with Lupin and

Gowing. I pressed him to have a little whisky, and he replied that he had given up whisky; but would like a little "Unsweetened," as he was advised it was the most healthy spirit. I had none in the house, but sent Sarah round to Lockwood's for some.

It may seem callous, but Gowing and I scooted to The Oyster and Fiddle and drank till closing time. After we had had four pints each, it was my turn to buy the next round.

"I'll just have a half," Gowing said – and laughed.

"What's funny," I asked.

"I do have a half," he giggled.

"No you don't," I pointed out. His glass was empty.

"Oh yes I do," he was by now well in his cups.

I was about to suggest we'd both had enough when he motioned me to sit close to him.

"Can you keep a secret," he whispered.

"Yes."

"I have a half. Half a shop."

Slowly and slurring some of time, he told me his whole story and why he had never said a word to Pa. He was afraid that Pa would be less friendly if he knew Gowing was half a shopkeeper rather than something in the City.

The City was not just then an enviable berth, in fact. The next day, when I got to the office, it was padlocked shut. As I feared, Job Cleanands had gone on the run to avoid his creditors, his customers and the police. He was acting in the best traditions of failed Stock Market men. The ones who succeed tend to become knights of the realm; the ones who fail have to duck and weave – and sometimes flee. Pa himself realised the truth the next morning:

February 20.—The first thing that caught my eye on opening the Standard was—"Great Failure of Stock and Share Dealers! Mr. Job Cleanands absconded!" I handed it to Carrie, and she replied: "Oh! perhaps it's for Lupin's good. I never did think it a suitable situation for him." I thought the whole affair very shocking.

Lupin came down to breakfast, and seeing he looked painfully distressed, I said: "We know the news, my dear boy, and feel very sorry for you." Lupin said: "How did you know? who told you?" I handed him the Standard. He threw the paper down, and said: "Oh I don't care a button for that! I expected that, but I did not expect this." He then read a letter from Frank Mutlar, announcing, in a cool manner, that Daisy Mutlar is to be married next month to Murray Posh. I exclaimed, "Murray Posh! Is not that the very man Frank had the impudence to bring here last Tuesday week?" Lupin said: "Yes; the 'Posh's-three-shilling-hats' chap."

We all then ate our breakfast in dead silence.

In fact, I could eat nothing. I was not only too worried, but I cannot and will not eat cushion of bacon.

When Lupin rose to go I noticed a malicious smile creep over his face.

Malicious? How unkind that was of Pa who asked me what it meant. I replied: "Oh! only a little consolation—still it is a consolation. I have just remembered that, by my advice, Mr. Murray Posh has invested £600 in Parachikka Chlorates!"

March 20.—To-day being the day on which Daisy Mutlar and Mr. Murray Posh are to be married, Lupin has gone with a friend to spend the day at Gravesend.

There was no friend. I went alone. In Gravesend I consoled myself in the simplest of ways. I got drunk. I managed to totter on to the late train and fell asleep. I dreamed Daisy was still not that keen on intimacies, and so, Mr Murray Posh spent the first night of his marriage under the bed in a state of acute frustration. I did not awake when the Gravesend puffer pulled into Charing Cross. A hefty policeman shook me up.

"You're drunk and disorderly," he barked.

"I am sorry, sir. Troubles with women."

"Don't have anything to do with them … that's my advice."

"They don't even kiss you properly and then they marry someone else."

"You chose a weird one. Do you have a ticket?"

"I ate it," I said.

"I could charge you not just with travelling illegally but wolfing down railway property," he boomed.

I burped.

"Hop it," he said, "and count yourself lucky."

It's a good thing railway stations have washrooms. For sixpence I washed and brushed myself up. I then ate six mints so my breath would not stink of booze and took a hansom home.

Sarah opened the door.

"You look dreadful. We've all been worried about you," she said.

"Why?"

"You're a silly mule." She dragged me in to the parlour.

"The prodigal returns," said Pa.

"It must have been a bad day," Ma said.

"He's well out of it," said Sarah.

"How dare you comment on my son's disappointment," Pa said.

"He doesn't seem to mind Mr Pooter, sir," Sarah said.

"She's right Pa. She's right. I think I'll stumble to bed."

Even stumbling was going to be an achievement.

"He has to see Mr Perkupp tomorrow," Pa said.

"A good night's sleep and a bath and he'll be fine," Ma said.

"I don't want him to disgrace himself in front of Mr Perkupp."

"He won't and he won't disgrace you," Ma said. "Sometimes Sarah you have to be firm with men."

Pa did not record this sudden outburst of feminist defiance. In his diary, he just said:

Lupin has been much cut-up over the affair, although he declares that he is glad it is off. I wish he would not go to so many music-halls, but one dare not say anything to him about it. At the present moment he irritates me by singing all over the house some nonsense about "What's the matter with Gladstone? He's all right! What's the matter with Lupin? He's all right!" I don't think either of them is. In the evening Gowing called, and the chief topic of conversation was Daisy's marriage to Murray Posh. I said: "I was glad the matter was at an end, as Daisy would only have made a fool of Lupin." Gowing, with his usual good taste, said: "Oh, Master Lupin can make a fool of himself without any assistance." Carrie very properly resented this, and Gowing had sufficient sense to say he was sorry.

Carrie was all of a tremble when she read the letter, and all she could keep on saying was: "Oh, I do hope it will be all right." For myself, I could scarcely eat any breakfast. Lupin came down dressed quietly, and looking a perfect gentleman, except that his face was rather yellow. Carrie, by way of encouragement said: "You do look nice, Lupin." Lupin replied: "Yes, it's a good make-up, isn't it? A regular-downright-respectable-funereal-first-class-City-firm-junior-clerk." He laughed rather ironically.

In the hall I heard a great noise, and also Lupin shouting to Sarah to fetch down his old hat. I went into the passage, and found Lupin in a fury, kicking and smashing a new tall hat. I said: "Lupin, my boy, what are you doing? How wicked of you! Some poor fellow would be glad to have it." Lupin replied: "I would not insult any poor fellow by giving it to him."

When he had gone outside, I picked up the battered hat, and saw inside "Posh's Patent." Poor Lupin! I can forgive him. It seemed hours before we reached the office. Mr. Perkupp sent for Lupin, who was with him nearly an hour. He returned, as I

Mr Murray Posh

thought, crestfallen in appearance. I said: "Well, Lupin, how about Mr. Perkupp?"

Lupin commenced his song: "What's the matter with Perkupp? He's all right!"

I sang of the glories of Perkupp because Pa was trying to help me, after all. And I knew it would please him.

I felt instinctively my boy was engaged. I went to Mr. Perkupp, but I could not speak. He said: "Well, Mr. Pooter, what is it?" I must have looked a fool, for all I could say was: "Mr. Perkupp, you are a good man." He looked at me for a moment, and said: "No, Mr. Pooter, you are the good man; and we'll see if we cannot get your son to follow such an excellent example." I said: "Mr. Perkupp, may I go home? I cannot work any more to-day."

'My good master', Pa went on to say. As I read the phrase I could scream in protest. For 21 years Pa had slaved and contributed to the profits of the firm, and yet, he thought of Perkupp as his good master. Yes sir, no sir, three bags full sir. Alienation Marx called it. But Pa was deeply grateful as Perkupp shook his hand warmly and then, the sadly unaware slave praised his master for being so kind. I wanted to shake Pa into standing up for himself but instead Pa crawled.

It was as much as I could do to prevent myself from crying in the 'bus; in fact, I should have done so, had my thoughts not been interrupted by Lupin, who was having a quarrel with a fat man in the 'bus, whom he accused of taking up too much room.

I've just done what Pa wanted, but instead of understanding that I had to quash something in me to finally work under Perkupp, Pa found spurious reason to complain. The fat man was pushing me off the seat. Don't tell me fathers are perfect or perfectly grown up. By the evening, at least, we had become calmer.

In the evening Carrie sent round for dear old friend Cummings and his wife, and also to Gowing. We all sat round the fire, and got in a bottle of "Jackson Frères," which Sarah fetched from the grocer's, drank Lupin's health. I lay awake for hours, thinking of the future. My boy in the same office as myself—we can go down together by the 'bus, come home together, and who knows but in the course of time he may take great interest in our little home. That he may help me to put a nail in here or a nail in there, or help his dear mother to hang a picture. In the summer he may help us in our little garden with the flowers, and assist us to paint the stands and pots. (By-the-by, I must get in some more enamel paint.) All this I thought over and over again, and a thousand happy thoughts beside. I heard the clock strike four, and soon after fell asleep, only to dream of three happy people—Lupin, dear Carrie, and myself.

Very sweet of Pa. I did not dare tell him I would flee from Perkupp as soon as I could.

Pa's diary now introduced a character who was to play something of a large part in our lives. On May 10, Pa and Ma were invited to dinner at Franching's to meet Mr. Hardfur Huttle whose name, with its mention of furs, makes me think of Eskimos. But to Pa the guests were anything but Arctic wild men.

I must say it was quite a distinguished party, and although we did not know anybody personally, they all seemed to be quite swells.

Pa swelled up at the idea of being near swells – and Hardfur Huttle was not merely a swell, but a rather learned swell. Pa wrote:

Mr. Hardfur Huttle did all the talking. He is a marvellously intellectual man and says things which from other people would seem quite alarming. How I wish I could remember even a quarter of his brilliant conversation. I made a few little reminding notes on the menu card.

One observation struck me as being absolutely powerful—though not to my way of thinking of course. Mrs. Purdick happened to say "You are certainly unorthodox, Mr. Huttle." Mr. Huttle, with a peculiar expression (I can see it now) said in a slow rich voice: "Mrs. Purdick, 'orthodox' is a grandiloquent word implying sticking-in-the-mud. If Columbus and Stephenson had been orthodox, there would neither have been the discovery of America nor the steam-engine." There was quite a silence. It appeared to me that such teaching was absolutely dangerous, and yet I felt—in fact we must all have felt—there was no answer to the argument. A little later on, Mrs. Purdick, who is Franching's sister and also acted as hostess, rose from the table, and Mr. Huttle said: "Why, ladies, do you deprive us of your company so soon? Why not wait while we have our cigars?"

Hardfur Huttle

The effect was electrical. The ladies (including Carrie) were in no way inclined to be deprived of Mr. Huttle's fascinating society, and immediately resumed their seats, amid much laughter and a little chaff. Mr. Huttle said: "Well, that's a real good sign; you shall not be insulted by being called orthodox any longer." Mrs. Purdick, who seemed to be a bright and rather sharp woman, said: "Mr. Huttle, we will meet you half-way—that is, till you get half-way through your cigar. That, at all events, will be the happy medium."

I shall never forget the effect the words, "happy medium," had upon him. He was brilliant and most daring in his interpretation of the words. He positively alarmed me.

When I first read this in the diary I did not think that much about Pa's alarm but the more I think about him, the more telling it seems. Hardfur Huttle had no intention of praising the happy medium, which was what Pa admired because it seemed safe.

He (Hardfur) said something like the following: "Happy medium, indeed. Do you know 'happy medium' are two words which mean 'miserable mediocrity'? I say, go first class or third; marry a duchess or her kitchen maid. The happy medium means respectability, and respectability means insipidness. Does it not, Mr. Pooter?"

I was so taken aback by being personally appealed to, that I could only bow apologetically, and say I feared I was not competent to offer an opinion. Carrie was about to say something; but she was interrupted, for which I was rather pleased, for she is not clever at argument, and one has to be extra clever to discuss a subject with a man like Mr. Huttle.

The real reason Ma was tempted to say something and then stopped was that her own mother was an under maid and that she had only had a very basic education. Anything that reminded her of that made Ma very embarrassed. It was only with Pa that she had a real confidence which meant, of course, they had a good marriage. For his part, Pa was dazzled by Hardfur as well as alarmed.

He continued, with an amazing eloquence that made his unwelcome opinions positively convincing: "The happy medium is nothing more or less than a vulgar half-measure. A man who loves champagne and, finding a pint too little, fears to face a whole bottle and has recourse to an imperial pint, will never build a Brooklyn Bridge or an Eiffel Tower. No, he is half-hearted, he is a half-measure—respectable—in fact, a happy medium, and will spend the rest of his days in a suburban villa with a stucco-column portico, resembling a four-post bedstead."

We all laughed.

"That sort of thing," continued Mr. Huttle, "belongs to a soft man, with a soft beard with a soft head, with a made tie that hooks on."

Again Pa took this as an attack. I wish there were pills for paranoia; I would have rushed to the pharmacy to get a large bottle for Pa, who admitted:

This seemed rather personal and twice I caught myself looking in the glass of the cheffonière; for I had on a tie that hooked on—and why not? If these remarks were not personal they were rather careless, and so were some of his subsequent observations, which must have made both Mr. Franching and his guests rather uncomfortable. I don't think Mr. Huttle meant to be personal, for he added: "We don't know that class here in this country: but we do in America, and I've no use for them."

Franching several times suggested that the wine should be passed round the table, which Mr. Huttle did not heed; but continued as if he were giving a lecture:

"What we want in America is your homes. We live on wheels. Your simple, quiet life and home, Mr. Franching, are charming. No display, no pretension! You make no difference in your dinner, I dare say, when you sit down by yourself and when you invite us. You have your own personal attendant—no hired waiter to breathe on the back of your head."

I saw Franching palpably wince at this.

Mr. Huttle continued: "Just a small dinner with a few good things, such as you have this evening. You don't insult your guests by sending to the grocer for champagne at six shillings a bottle."

I could not help thinking of "Jackson Frères" at three-and-six!

"In fact," said Mr. Huttle, "a man is little less than a murderer who does. That is the province of the milksop, who wastes his evening at home playing dominoes with his wife. I've heard of these people. We don't want them at this table. Our party is well selected. We've no use for deaf old women, who cannot follow intellectual conversation."

All our eyes were turned to Mrs. Field, who fortunately, being deaf, did not hear his remarks; but continued smiling approval.

"We have no representative at Mr. Franching's table," said Mr. Huttle, "of the unenlightened frivolous matron, who goes to a second class dance at Bayswater and fancies she is in Society. Society does not know her; it has no use for her."

Mr. Huttle paused for a moment and the opportunity was afforded for the ladies to rise. I asked Mr. Franching quietly to excuse me, as I did not wish to miss the last train, which we very nearly did, by-the-by, through Carrie having mislaid the little cloth cricket-cap which she wears when we go out.

It was very late when Carrie and I got home; but on entering the sitting-room I said: "Carrie, what do you think of Mr. Hardfur Huttle?" She simply answered: "How like Lupin!" The same idea occurred to me in the train. The comparison kept me awake half the night. Mr. Huttle was, of course, an older and more influential man; but he was like Lupin, and it made me think how dangerous Lupin would be if he were older and more influential.

When I read this I see Pa saw me as an anarchist, but to be fair, he did not just linger on the dangers I might pose to world for he continued:

I feel proud to think Lupin does resemble Mr. Huttle in some ways. Lupin, like Mr. Huttle, has original and sometimes wonderful ideas; but it is those ideas that are so dangerous. They make men extremely rich or extremely poor. They make or break men. I always feel people are happier who live a simple unsophisticated life. I believe I am happy because I am not ambitious. Somehow I feel that Lupin, since he has been with Mr. Perkupp, has become content to settle down and follow the footsteps of his father. This is a comfort.

Comfort was short lived. The next day the offices of Perkupp's grim enterprise were rather empty. Our chief of men had disappeared and I now wondered whether he was in the habit of refreshing himself at Madame Romanova's with Ludmila from Poplar or Anouchka from Epping. Pa was ill. The senior clerk revelled in the freedom of Perkupp's absence and had fallen asleep. He was snoring loudly and dribbling over a ledger. It was at this moment that a tall man strode into our office.

"A hive of activity, I see," the tall man sneered. "Where is Mr Perkupp? Or is he also asleep?"

Someone had to speak up. "I'm afraid he's out, sir."

"Is he out drumming up business?"

"I expect so," I said.

"You are an optimist. You work here?"

"Lupin Pooter at your service, sir."

"I didn't ask your name, young man. I asked if you worked here."

"I do, sir."

"What are you doing?"

"I can hardly reveal that to someone who has just walked off the street."

"My name is Crowbillon … I see you do not know my name."

"Of course, I know your name. You're a treasured customer, sir."

"Not treasured enough, I think."

"Perhaps you could tell me what is troubling you, sir?"

"You're not as stupid as you look. Something is troubling me, indeed. And what troubles me soon will be troubling Perkupp much more. He is a disgrace to business."

Crowbillon spoke with ferocity. He too was clearly not a happy medium man.

"I'm sure Mr Perkupp won't mind us sitting in his office and perhaps you can tell me what is on your mind."

"Perkupp's mind or rather his lack of mind. The mind that does not whirl, scheme and analyse all the time is unlikely to make profit. The lack of profit is on my mind."

"Are you unhappy with the way we have conducted your account, sir?"

"Unhappy doesn't begin to cover it."

"Mr Perkupp will be most upset but I can understand your point of view."

"How old are you?"

"Twenty."

"How old do you think I am?"

"I've no idea but you're clearly a man of experience."

"Flattery does not work with me," he smiled menacingly.

"Then you are a rare man," I told him.

He did not acknowledge the compliment.

"Won't your boss mind you sitting in his chair?"

"I don't know but in my limited experience what bosses really mind is if you make suggestions."

"What kind of suggestions," Crowbillon asked sharply.

"In my previous work I made suggestions which might boost profits."

"And what did your superiors say?"

"They did not like it."

I could not tell if he approved or disapproved but some diabolo made me go on. "I turned up the next day wearing a dog muzzle so I wouldn't make any more unwelcome suggestions."

Crowbillon laughed. "Ingenious," he added, "and enough to drive most bosses mad."

"He chucked me out. Just for making a suggestion."

Crowbillon laughed again. "Was it a good suggestion?"

"As it was never tested I don't know. I made it in good faith."

"And hoping to impress your superior?"

"He is now engaged to a bar girl who sells more than beer. And he's taken to wearing a wig."

"You don't think much of him," Crowbillon observed.

"Does it show?"

"You know it shows. And what do you think of Perkupp?"

"I have only been working for him for a week."

"And you don't want to seem disloyal?"

"Yes … well," I hesitated.

"He who hesitates is lost, young man. I never hesitate."

Crowbillon made for the door. I stopped hesitating. "Your drift isn't entirely lost on me. You're obviously not entirely happy with our services, sir."

"At least you're not a total moron. Perkupp is fifty years out of date and has not had a new idea since Disraeli bought the Suez Canal. What this place needs is a total revolution."

"Revolution would frighten Mr Perkupp, sir."

"He needs to be frightened."

"Perhaps I can make a suggestion, sir."

"You seem to like making suggestions, young man. I hope it's a revolutionary one."

"Certainly not no, no," I laughed. I did not want the rest of the clerks to hear. "Well, perhaps a little."

You will get some sense of the conversation that followed between Crowbillon and myself from Pa's diary.

May 13.—A terrible misfortune has happened: Lupin is discharged from Mr. Perkupp's office; and I scarcely know how I am writing my diary. I was away from office last Sat., the first time I have been absent through illness for twenty years. I believe I was poisoned by some lobster. Mr. Perkupp was also absent, as Fate would have it; and our most valued customer, Mr. Crowbillon, went to the office in a rage, and withdrew his custom. My boy Lupin not only had the assurance to receive him, but recommended him the firm of Gylterson, Sons and Co. Limited. In my own humble judgment, and though I have to say it against my own son, this seems an act of treachery.

This morning I receive a letter from Perkupp, informing me that Lupin's services are no longer required, and an interview with me is desired at eleven o'clock. I went down to the office with an aching heart, dreading an interview with Mr. Perkupp, with whom I have never had a word. I saw nothing of Lupin in the morning. He had not got up when it was time for me to leave, and Carrie said I should do no good by disturbing him. My mind wandered so at the office that I could not do my work properly.

As I expected, I was sent for by Mr. Perkupp, and the following conversation ensued as nearly as I can remember it.

Mr. Perkupp said: "Good-morning, Mr. Pooter! This is a very serious business. I am not referring so much to the dismissal of your son, for I knew we should have to part sooner or later. I am the head of this old, influential, and much-respected firm; and when I consider the time has come to revolutionise the business, I will do it myself."

I could see my good master was somewhat affected, and I said: "I hope, sir, you do not imagine that I have in any way countenanced my son's unwarrantable interference?" Mr. Perkupp rose from his seat and took my hand, and said: "Mr. Pooter, I would as soon suspect myself as suspect you." I was so agitated that in the confusion, to show my gratitude I very nearly called him a "grand old man."

This was the phrase used to describe William Gladstone who first became Prime Minister in 1868 and was still in 10 Downing Street nearly thirty years later, though he had occasionally had to cede the premises to Benjamin Disraeli. As he said Pa managed not to utter the phrase 'grand old man'.

Fortunately I checked myself in time, and said he was a "grand old master." I was so unaccountable for my actions that I sat down, leaving him standing. Of course, I at once rose, but Mr. Perkupp bade me sit down, which I was very pleased to do. Mr. Perkupp, resuming, said: "You will understand, Mr. Pooter, that the high-standing nature of our firm will not admit of our bending to anybody. If Mr. Crowbillon chooses to put his work into other hands—I may add, less experienced hands—it is not for us to bend and beg back his custom."

"You shall not do it, sir," I said with indignation.

"Exactly," replied Mr. Perkupp; "I shall not do it. But I was thinking this, Mr. Pooter. Mr. Crowbillon is our most valued client, and I will even confess—for I know this will not go beyond ourselves—that we cannot afford very well to lose him, especially in these times, which are not of the brightest. Now, I fancy you can be of service."

I replied: "Mr. Perkupp, I will work day and night to serve you!"

Mr. Perkupp said: "I know you will. Now, what I should like you to do is this. You yourself might write to Mr. Crowbillon—you must not, of course, lead him to suppose I know anything about your doing so—and explain to him that your son was only taken on as a clerk—quite an inexperienced one in fact—out of the respect the firm had for you, Mr. Pooter. This is, of course, a fact. I don't suggest that you should speak in too strong terms of your own son's conduct; but I may add, that had he been a son of mine, I should have condemned his interference with no measured terms. That I leave to you. I think the result will be that Mr. Crowbillon will see the force of the foolish step he has taken, and our firm will neither suffer in dignity nor in pocket."

Pa, of course, took Perkupp's side against me. He slaved over the letter and went to lavish praise on his saintly superior. I was an inexperienced young lout who had no business making business suggestions. Perkupp was himself utterly confident of Pa's loyalty. If he had told Pa to take me up to the top of Mt Ararat and skewer me as the Lord instructed Abraham to skewer Isaac, I've no doubt Pa would have complied. Luckily it didn't come to that but Pa's 'my master is perfect' tone still makes me ill. Pa grovelled:

I could not help thinking what a noble gentleman Mr. Perkupp is. His manners and his way of speaking seem to almost thrill one with respect.

I said: "Would you like to see the letter before I send it?"

Mr. Perkupp said: "Oh no! I had better not. I am supposed to know nothing about it, and I have every confidence in you. You must write the letter carefully. We are not very busy; you had better take the morning tomorrow, or the whole day if you like. I shall be here myself all day tomorrow, in fact all the week, in case Mr. Crowbillon should call."

I decided I would not treat my dismissal as a tragedy. The City had plenty of jobs for bright young men though I knew that Perkupp would never give me a letter of recommendation. Pa himself only saw me a young hound like Down had done and, worse, a young hound who wore unsuitable headgear.

Lupin came into the parlour for a moment with a new hat

on, and asked my opinion of it. I said I was not in the mood to judge of hats, and I did not think he was in a position to buy a new one. Lupin replied carelessly: "I didn't buy it; it was a present."

I have such terrible suspicions of Lupin now that I scarcely like to ask him questions, as I dread the answers so. He, however, saved me the trouble.

He said: "I met a friend, an old friend, that I did not quite think a friend at the time; but it's all right. As he wisely said, 'all is fair in love and war,' and there was no reason why we should not be friends still. He's a jolly, good, all-round sort of fellow, and a very different stamp from that inflated fool of a Perkupp."

I said: "Hush, Lupin! Do not pray add insult to injury."

Lupin said: "What do you mean by injury? I repeat, I have done no injury. Crowbillon is simply tired of a stagnant stick-in-the-mud firm, and made the change on his own account. I simply recommended the new firm as a matter of biz—good old biz!"

Business did not work so good and please don't, as Pa would have done, remind me I'd murdered grammar. The crash of 1893 meant new thinking was required. Crowbillon realised it as Pa and Perkupp refused to do. Pa had to have a snap back and said:

"I don't understand your slang, and at my time of life have no desire to learn it; so, Lupin, my boy, let us change the subject. I will, if it please you, try and be interested in your new hat adventure."

Lupin said: "Oh! there's nothing much about it, except I have not once seen him since his marriage, and he said he was very pleased to see me, and hoped we should be friends. I stood a drink to cement the friendship, and he stood me a new hat—one of his own."

I said rather wearily: "But you have not told me your old friend's name?"

Lupin said, with affected carelessness: "Oh didn't I? Well, I will. It was Murray Posh."

If it were not for Posh and his hats, I might have married Daisy and spent years bickering over intimacies, so I suppose I owe hats something.

May 14.—Lupin came down late, and seeing me at home all the morning, asked the reason of it. Carrie and I both agreed it was better to say nothing to him about the letter I was writing, so I evaded the question.

Lupin went out, saying he was going to lunch with Murray Posh in the City. I said I hoped Mr. Posh would provide him with a berth. Lupin went out laughing, saying: "I don't mind wearing Posh's one-priced hats, but I am not going to sell them." Poor boy, I fear he is perfectly hopeless.

Pa made much of the fact that he was trying to mend fences with Crowbillon which I could have told him was hopeless and would only expose him to humiliation. He came home late from the office having sent Ma a note not to wait for him for dinner. The poor man had been noting all day, he admitted.

It took me nearly the whole day to write to Mr. Crowbillon. Once or twice I asked Carrie for suggestions; and although it seems ungrateful, her suggestions were none of them to the point, while one or two were absolutely idiotic. Of course I did not tell her so. I got the letter off, and took it down to the office for Mr. Perkupp to see, but he again repeated that he could trust me.

Gowing called in the evening, and I was obliged to tell him about Lupin and Mr. Perkupp; and, to my surprise, he was quite inclined to side with Lupin. Carrie joined in, and said she thought I was taking much too melancholy a view of it. Gowing produced a pint sample-bottle of Madeira, which had been given him, which he said would get rid of the blues. I dare say it would have done so if there had been more of it; but as Gowing helped himself to three glasses, it did not leave much for Carrie and me to get rid of the blues with.

Earlier Pa had dismissed the term the "blues" as one of my blithering slang words. In fact, it had been used for three centuries and so was nothing new. In the 1600s, it referred to the "...intense visual hallucinations that can accompany severe alcohol withdrawal". Eventually, the phrase came to mean a state of depression. By the 1800s in the US, the term "blues" was associated with drinking alcohol.

When Pa went to work that day, he didn't just have the blues but the jitters too. He was in a blue funk, in fact.

May 15.—A day of great anxiety, for I expected every moment a letter from Mr. Crowbillon. Two letters came in the evening—one for me, with "Crowbillon Hall" printed in large gold-

and-red letters on the back of the envelope; the other for Lupin, which I felt inclined to open and read, as it had "Gylterson, Sons, and Co. Limited," which was the recommended firm. I trembled as I opened Mr. Crowbillon's letter. I wrote him sixteen pages, closely written; he wrote me less than sixteen lines.

His letter was: "Sir,—I totally disagree with you. Your son, in the course of five minutes' conversation, displayed more intelligence than your firm has done during the last five years.—Yours faithfully, Gilbert E. Gillam O. Crowbillon."

Pa should have been proud of me, but he was nothing of the sort. I was tempted to tell him Perkupp was a patron of the Palace of Russian Beauties and that his reputation at Madame Romanova's was of a fellow who liked to partake of his pleasures. If she'd charged me ten quid, I wonder what she charged him. But if I raised that question, Pa would guess I'd poddled a Russian girl there. And he'd be bound to tell Ma. So I said nothing. He struggled as he could not decide what to do – and for once he was totally honest.

What am I to do? Here is a letter that I dare not show to Mr. Perkupp, and would not show to Lupin for anything. The crisis had yet to come; for Lupin arrived, and, opening his letter, showed a cheque for £25 as a commission for the recommendation of Mr. Crowbillon, whose custom to Mr. Perkupp is evidently lost for ever. Cummings and Gowing both called, and both took Lupin's part. Cummings went so far as to say that Lupin would make a name yet. I suppose I was melancholy, for I could only ask: "Yes, but what sort of a name?"

Typically Pa imagined that the name I was most likely to have attached was a dishonourable one. Lupin the louse, Lupin the liar, but these were better than Lupin the loser. Eventually Pa compromised with his conscience, as he admitted.

May 16.—I told Mr. Perkupp the contents of the letter in a modified form, but Mr. Perkupp said: "Pray don't discuss the matter; it is at an end. Your son will bring his punishment upon himself." I went home in the evening, thinking of the hopeless future of Lupin. I found him in most extravagant spirits and in evening dress. He threw a letter on the table for me to read.

Hopeless future indeed. Perkupp had predicted I would bring punishment on myself. His prediction was as wrong as his predictions of what shares to buy. I have to admit that I knew that when Pa read the letter I threw down on the table, he wouldn't, he couldn't, be pleased. The triumph of the son is indeed the downfall of the father. Pa was, in fact, flabbergasted.

To my amazement, I read that Gylterson and Sons had absolutely engaged Lupin at a salary of £200 a year, with other advantages. I read the letter through three times and thought it must have been for me. But there it was—Lupin Pooter—plain enough. I was silent. Lupin said: "What price Perkupp now? You take my tip, Guv.—'off' with Perkupp and freeze on to Gylterson, the firm of the future! Perkupp's firm? The stagnant dummies have been standing still for years, and now are moving back. I want to go on. In fact I must go off, as I am dining with the Murray Poshs to-night."

In the exuberance of his spirits he hit his hat with his stick, gave a loud war "Whoo-oop," jumped over a chair, and took the liberty of rumpling my hair all over my forehead, and bounced out of the room, giving me no chance of reminding him of his age and the respect which was due to his parent. Gowing and Cummings came in the evening, and positively cheered me up with congratulations respecting Lupin.

Gowing said: "I always said he would get on, and, take my word, he has more in his head than we three put together."

Carrie said: "He is a second Hardfur Huttle."

This picture was apparently taken in an asylum in 1890. I wonder what became of them all. The girl at the bottom reminds me of my Oldham Rosie.

Hardfur Huttle was the swell who had read so much. Pa never expected to see him again, let alone hear from him. Ironically though I was now safe Pa found my company hard to bear.

Between the middle of May and the end of June, Pa wrote nothing. For him nothing happened but, for me, it was a critical period. I decided that the time had come to leave my parents' house. For any young man that is a big decision but I felt I would always behave like a child in a house where my father especially treated me as a child.

July 1.—I find, on looking over my diary, nothing of any consequence has taken place during the last month. To-day we lose Lupin, who has taken furnished apartments at Bayswater, near his friends, Mr. and Mrs. Murray Posh, at two guineas a week. I think this is most extravagant of him, as it is half his salary. Lupin says one never loses by a good address, and, to use his own expression, Brickfield Terrace is a bit "off." Whether he means it is "far off" I do not know. I have long since given up trying to understand his curious expressions. I said the neighbourhood had always been good enough for his parents. His reply was: "It is no question of being good or bad. There is no money in it, and I am not going to rot away my life in the suburbs."

We are sorry to lose him, but perhaps he will get on better by himself, and there may be some truth in his remark that an old and a young horse can't pull together in the same cart.

Gowing called, and said that the house seemed quite peaceful, and like old times. He liked Master Lupin very well, but he occasionally suffered from what he could not help—youth.

July 3, Sunday.—In the afternoon, as I was looking out of the parlour window, which was open, a grand trap, driven by a lady, with a gentleman seated by the side of her, stopped at our door. Not wishing to be seen, I withdrew my head very quickly, knocking the back of it violently against the sharp edge of the window-sash. I was nearly stunned. There was a loud double-knock at the front door; Carrie rushed out of the parlour, upstairs to her room, and I followed, as Carrie thought it was Mr. Perkupp. I thought it was Mr. Franching.—I whispered to Sarah over the bannisters: "Show them into the drawing-room." Sarah said, as the shutters were not opened, the room would smell musty. There was another loud rat-tat. I whispered: "Then show them into the parlour, and say Mr. Pooter will be down directly." I changed my coat, but could not see to do my hair, as Carrie was occupying the glass.

Sarah came up, and said it was Mrs. Murray Posh and Mr. Lupin.

This was quite a relief. I went down with Carrie, and Lupin met me with the remark: "I say, what did you run away from the window for? Did we frighten you?"

I foolishly said: "What window?"

Lupin said: "Oh, you know. Shut it. You looked as if you were playing at Punch and Judy."

On Carrie asking if she could offer them anything, Lupin said: "Oh, I think Daisy will take on a cup of tea. I can do with a B. and S."

I said: "I am afraid we have no soda."

Lupin said: "Don't bother about that. You just trip out and hold the horse; I don't think Sarah understands it."

Once, of course, I'd never have dared speak like that to Pa, but I was no longer under his roof.

"Of course I understand the horse. It's an animal isn't it?" Sarah shot me a look; "I'm good with animals as you know."

"What did she mean by that," Pa asked.

"It's just a remark," Ma said as Sarah walked out.

Pa was relieved we did not linger.

They stayed a very short time, and as they were leaving, Lupin said: "I want you both to come and dine with me next Wednesday, and see my new place. Mr. and Mrs. Murray Posh, Miss Posh (Murray's sister) are coming. Eight o'clock sharp. No one else."

I said we did not pretend to be fashionable people, and would like the dinner earlier, as it made it so late before we got home.

Lupin said: "Rats! You must get used to it. If it comes to that, Daisy and I can drive you home."

We promised to go; but I must say in my simple mind the familiar way in which Mrs. Posh and Lupin addressed each other is reprehensible. Anybody would think they had been children together. I certainly should object to a six months' acquaintance calling my wife "Carrie," and driving out with her.

Daisy and I had not been children together but we had been engaged. I was surprised by the fact that I did not feel either jealousy or regret. As a friend, however, Daisy was fine. As were my new rooms which even Pa had to admit:

July 4.—Lupin's rooms looked very nice; but the dinner was, I thought, a little too grand, especially as he commenced with champagne straight off. I also think Lupin might have told us that he and Mr. and Mrs. Murray Posh and Miss Posh were going to put on full evening dress. Knowing that the dinner was only for us six, we never dreamed it would be a full dress affair. I had no appetite. It was quite twenty minutes past eight before we sat down to dinner. At six I could have eaten a hearty meal. I had a bit of bread-and-butter at that hour, feeling famished, and I expect that partly spoiled my appetite.

We were introduced to Miss Posh, whom Lupin called "Lillie Girl," as if he had known her all his life. She was very tall, rather plain, and I thought she was a little painted round the eyes. I hope I am wrong; but she had such fair hair, and yet her eyebrows were black. She looked about thirty. I did not like the way she kept giggling and giving Lupin smacks and pinching him. Then her laugh was a sort of a scream that went right through my ears, all the more irritating because there was nothing to laugh at. In fact, Carrie and I were not at all prepossessed with her. They all smoked cigarettes after dinner, including Miss Posh, who startled Carrie by saying: "Don't you smoke, dear?" I answered for Carrie, and said: "Mrs. Charles Pooter has not arrived at it yet," whereupon Miss Posh gave one of her piercing laughs again.

Mrs. Posh sang a dozen songs at least, and I can only repeat what I have said before—she does not sing in tune; but Lupin sat by the side of the piano, gazing into her eyes the whole time. If I had been Mr. Posh, I think I should have had something to say about it. Mr. Posh made himself very agreeable to us, and eventually sent us home in his carriage, which I thought most kind. He is evidently very rich, for Mrs. Posh had on some beautiful jewellery. She told Carrie her necklace, which her husband gave her as a birthday present, alone cost £300.

Mr. Posh said he had a great belief in Lupin, and thought he would make rapid way in the world.

I could not help thinking of the £600 Mr. Posh lost over the Parachikka Chlorates through Lupin's advice.

During the evening I had an opportunity to speak to Lupin, and expressed a hope that Mr. Posh was not living beyond his means.

Lupin sneered, and said Mr. Posh was worth thousands. "Posh's one-price hat" was a household word in Birmingham, Manchester, Liverpool, and all the big towns throughout England. Lupin further informed me that Mr. Posh was opening branch establishments at New York, Sydney, and Melbourne, and was negotiating for Kimberley and Johannesburg.

I said I was pleased to hear it.

Lupin said: "Why, he has settled over £10,000 on Daisy, and the same amount on 'Lillie Girl.' If at any time I wanted a little capital, he would put up a couple of 'thou' at a day's notice, and could buy up Perkupp's firm over his head at any moment with ready cash."

On the way home in the carriage, for the first time in my life, I was inclined to indulge in the radical thought that money was not properly divided.

I could have told Pa that he was being sensible for once. We live in an unfair world. Most of the rich don't deserve their riches and most of the poor don't deserve their poverty. Perkupp had inherited his position because his father owned the firm and had, in fact, asked to be buried with one of his ledgers. Pa, at least, with his new salary could allow himself the comfort of a cab. It was not to be the last cab he took that night.

On arriving home at a quarter-past eleven, we found a hansom cab, which had been waiting for me for two hours with a letter. Sarah said she did not know what to do, as we had not left the address where we had gone. I trembled as I opened the letter, fearing it was some bad news about Mr. Perkupp. The note was: "Dear Mr. Pooter,—Come down to the Victoria Hotel without delay. Important. Yours truly, Hardfur Huttle."

I asked the cabman if it was too late. The cabman replied that it was not; for his instructions were, if I happened to be out, he was to wait till I came home. I felt very tired, and really wanted to go to bed. I reached the hotel at a quarter before midnight. I apologised for being so late, but Mr. Huttle said: "Not at all; come and have a few oysters." I feel my heart beating as I write these words. To be brief, Mr. Huttle said he had a rich American friend who wanted to do something large in our line of business, and that Mr. Franching had mentioned my name to him. We talked over the matter. If, by any happy chance, the result be successful, I can more than compensate my dear master for the loss of Mr. Crowbillon's custom. Mr. Huttle had previously said: "The glorious 'Fourth' is a lucky day for America, and, as it has not yet struck twelve, we will celebrate it with a glass of the best wine to be had in the place, and drink good luck to our bit of business."

I fervently hope it will bring good luck to us all.

It was two o'clock when I got home. Although I was so tired, I could not sleep except for short intervals—then only to dream.

I kept dreaming of Mr. Perkupp and Mr. Huttle.

What would the new psychologists make of Pa's dreams? I think they would not find them too much of a challenge. He wore his unconscious on his sleeve. Hardfur, it seems, enraptured him even more than Perkupp which showed that, even when he was asleep, Pa had kept a minimum of marbles.

Mr Huttle was in a lovely palace with a crown on. Mr. Perkupp was waiting in the room. Mr. Huttle kept taking off this crown and handing it to me, and calling me "President."

I was pleased Pa wrote of himself as President as it showed he still had some ambition. If there is any conversation among the Highgate dead, he could discuss the iniquities of property with Karl Marx.

Mr. Huttle had previously said: "The glorious 'Fourth' is a lucky day for America, and, as it has not yet struck twelve, we will celebrate it with a glass of the best wine to be had in the place, and drink good luck to our bit of business."

I fervently hope it will bring good luck to us all.

It was two o'clock when I got home. Although I was so tired, I could not sleep except for short intervals—then only to dream.

I kept dreaming of Mr. Perkupp and Mr. Huttle. The latter was in a lovely palace with a crown on. Mr. Perkupp was waiting in the room. Mr. Huttle kept taking off this crown and handing it to me, and calling me "President."

He appeared to take no notice of Mr. Perkupp, and I kept asking Mr. Huttle to give the crown to my worthy master. Mr. Huttle kept saying: "No, this is the White House of Washington, and you must keep your crown, Mr. President."

We all laughed long and very loudly, till I got parched, and then I woke up. I fell asleep, only to dream the same thing over and over again.

The last few days had been momentous and I was pleased for myself and pleased for Pa, even though he found such turns of fortune unsettling as they were so different from the safe and steady he revered.

July 10.—The excitement and anxiety through which I have gone the last few days have been almost enough to turn my hair grey. It is all but settled. To-morrow the die will be cast. I have written a long letter to Lupin—feeling it my duty to do so,—regarding his attention to Mrs. Posh, for they drove up to our house again last night.

July 11.—I find my eyes filling with tears as I pen the note of my interview this morning with Mr. Perkupp. Addressing me, he said: "My faithful servant, I will not dwell on the important service you have done our firm. You can never be sufficiently thanked. Let us change the subject. Do you like your house, and are you happy where you are?"

I replied: "Yes, sir; I love my house and I love the neighbourhood, and could not bear to leave it."

Mr. Perkupp, to my surprise, said: "Mr. Pooter, I will purchase the freehold of that house, and present it to the most honest and most worthy man it has ever been my lot to meet."

He shook my hand, and said he hoped my wife and I would be spared many years to enjoy it. My heart was too full to thank him; and, seeing my embarrassment, the good fellow said: "You need say nothing, Mr. Pooter," and left the office.

I sent telegrams to Carrie, Gowing, and Cummings (a thing I have never done before), and asked the two latter to come round to supper.

On arriving home I found Carrie crying with joy, and I sent

Sarah round to the grocer's to get two bottles of "Jackson Frères."
My two dear friends came in the evening, and the last post brought a letter from Lupin in reply to mine. I read it aloud to them all. It ran: "My dear old Guv.,—Keep your hair on."

The phrase suggests, I fear, that Pa could remind me of bald man Down. I added:

You are on the wrong tack again. I am engaged to be married to 'Lillie Girl.' I did not mention it last Thursday, as it was not definitely settled. We shall be married in August, and amongst our guests we hope to see your old friends Gowing and Cummings. With much love to all, from The same old Lupin."

That was my last appearance in the diary. Pa obviously thought that was the sum of our relationship especially given I had signed myself 'the same old Lupin'. But, of course, I was beginning not to be the same old Lupin. One reason was that I had started reading, as I was troubled by Pa's perennial niggles. Was I partly to blame? Or was it just, as Pa said an old horse and a young horse find it hard to share the same cart. One of the books I read was the one I mentioned at the start by Edmund Gosse. It dealt with much the same subject as I am doing and so was of especial interest.

Gripe first. I can't help feeling that Gosse was encouraged by his father in a way I never was. He described how when he was eight, he started to write little monographs on seaside creatures, "*which were arranged, tabulated and divided as exactly as possible on the pattern of those which my Father was composing for his Actinologia Britannica. I wrote these out upon sheets of paper of the same size as his printed page, and I adorned them with water-colour plates, meant to emulate his precise and exquisite illustrations.*"

Gosse appreciated the way his father behaved.

But I can now well understand why my Father, very indulgently and good-temperedly, deprecated these exercises of mine. They took up, and, as he might well think, wasted, an enormous quantity of time; and they were, moreover, parodies, rather than imitations, of his writings, for I invented new species, with sapphire spots and crimson tentacles and amber bands, which were close enough to his real species to be disconcerting. He came from conscientiously shepherding the flocks of ocean, and I do not wonder that my ring-straked, speckled and spotted varieties put him out of countenance. If I had not been so innocent and solemn, he might have fancied I was mocking him.

Gosse's father used to come up to his Boxroom and try to talk to him. He also encouraged him to make friends so as "*he saw that I could not be allowed to spend my whole time in a little stuffy room making solemn and ridiculous imitations of Papers read before the Linnaean Society.*"

As he was had lost his mother, Gosse had to face a trial which I was spared:

"Very early one bright September morning at the close of my eleventh year, my Father called me over to him. I climbed up, and was snugly wrapped in the coverlid; and then we held a momentous conversation. It began abruptly by his asking me

whether I should like to have a new mamma. I was never a sentimentalist, and I therefore answered, cannily, that that would depend on who she was. He parried this, and announced that, anyway, a new mamma was coming; I was sure to like her.

Gosse's father was as worried about Miss Brightwen, his bride to be, coming as Pa had been about Perkupp visiting *The Laurels*. He insisted that the house should be in perfect order with no speck out of place. But the afternoon before she arrived was a dramatic one. Gosse wrote:

In the course of the afternoon. I was dancing about the drawing-room, and was saying: 'Oh! I am so glad my new Mamma is coming,' when Miss Marks called out, in an unnatural voice, 'Oh! you cruel child.' I stopped in amazement and stared at her, whereupon she threw prudence to the winds, and moaned: 'I once thought I should be your dear mamma.' I was simply stupefied, and I expressed my horror in terms that were clear and strong.

At *The Laurels* we had never experienced such scenes of jealousy. Gosse might as well have been in Othello by the Beach. Sarah and I, young as we were, had our tiffs quietly behind closed doors. Even after I got engaged to Daisy, Sarah behaved sensibly. Young Gosse had less luck.

Thereupon Miss Marks had a wild fit of hysterics, while I looked on, wholly unsympathetic and still deeply affronted. She was right; I was cruel, alas! but then, what a silly woman she had been! The consequence was that she withdrew in a moist and quivering condition to her boudoir, where she had locked herself in when I, all smiles and caresses, was welcoming the bride and bridegroom on the doorstep as politely as if I had been a valued old family retainer.

I was spared such scenes as Ma and Pa were respectably happy, an achievement given their own traumatic childhoods. And Pa was faithful. I could not have borne it if Ma died and Pa found a new wife. Gosse soon came to love his new mother, however. He wrote:

My stepmother immediately became a great ally of mine. She was never a tower of strength to me, but at least she was always a lodge in my garden of cucumbers.

I was never able to work out what Gosse meant by that extraordinary phrase. Was Gosse so cucumbered, by which I mean infatuated with cucumbers, that he picked a few, retreated into his lodge and chomped on them with a little salt and pepper? The older I get the more mysterious my fellow humans appear.

Pa adored Ma so he did not want to make her into a different woman. But Gosse's Pa saw his new wife as clay for him to mould. Young Gosse liked that because his father now had someone else to concentrate his energies on:

My Father, fully occupied with moulding the will and inflaming the piety of my stepmother, left me now, to a degree not precedented, in undisturbed possession of my own devices.

After his stepmother had been moulded, Gosse left the family home and was then subjected to a barrage of exhortations as his anxious father – fathers who care are anxious but that took me a long time to admit – deluged him daily with a *string of questions about conduct, its series of warnings, grew to be a burden which could hardly be borne, particularly because it involved a reply as punctual and if possible as full as itself. At the age of seventeen, the metaphysics of the soul are shadowy, and it is a dreadful thing to be forced to define the exact outline of what is so undulating and so shapeless.*

His father justified his behaviour by saying he had promised Gosse's mother to nurture his soul and, by that, he meant more than taking him to church and making sure he stayed awake during the sermon. Yet Gosse was generous – perhaps more generous than I have been as he went on to praise his father, saying:

I owe him a deep debt of gratitude for his beautiful faith in me in this respect, and now that I was alone in London, at this tender time of life, 'exposed', as they say, to all sorts of dangers, as defenceless as a fledgling that has been turned out of its nest, yet my Father did not, in his uplifted Quixotism, allow himself to fancy me guilty of any moral misbehaviour,

So different from my own Pa who, as his diary makes clear, was appalled by my hats, my suits and my behaviour. Though he never found out about my romantic adventures. Gosse was bothered by his father's intensity.

My holidays, however, and all my personal relations with my

Father were poisoned by this insistency. I was never at my ease in his company; I never knew when I might not be subjected to a series of searching questions which I should not be allowed to evade.

The questions were on a subject Pa never broached for old "Gosse" Perkupp was God himself. He asked if his son were "walking closely with God"? That made me think of young Gosse taking a stroll on some celestial cloud with the Almighty while his father whispered: "Don't ask any cheeky questions boy. And don't wear a muzzle." Do angels wear muzzles? No theologian seems to have considered the question but it seems unlikely as angels spend much of their time singing hymns.

Edmund Gosse and his family

Gosse kept on asking his father to leave him alone:

I demanded the right to think for myself, in which I repudiated the idea that my Father was responsible to God for my secret thoughts and my most intimate convictions.

Pa did not try to infiltrate my inner life, I will say that for him.

A book is a contract between the writer and the reader who has bought it and is ready to spend time reading it. As this is a father and son tale, I better not tail off, to imitate one of those puns Pa was so fond of, without rounding off my history.

For three years I went on working at Gytlerson's – and then decided to set up a small firm which specialised in risky foreign stocks, especially Russian and Turkish ones. I made a good deal of money and also joined, for I had been reading Marx avidly, the British Communist Party. If there was a revolution, I'd at least have shown some interest in the barricades. I did not tell Pa that I had joined for it would have upset him greatly.

In 1897, Pa was made a partner but the fortunes of the firm declined as Perfection Perkupp would not see that the world of finance changed as the century drew to a close. Pa and Ma continued to live in *The Laurels* but they had to get a new maid as Sarah left them to marry her beau Peters. I sent her a lavish wedding present as I'd always liked her.

Murray's sister, Little Posh and I got married too. I bought a house in Seymour Place, a fashionable street near Marble

Arch. At first we got on well, but she minded the fact that I worked long hours. She was more lonely than I imagined. I am sorry to say I was not very sympathetic, being more interested in the value of Siberian mines than my marriage.

In 1899, my secretary knocked on the door of my office in the City.

"A woman wants to see you. Shall I send her away?"

"Who is she?"

I saw at once who she was because she stood in the doorway. Sarah was smartly dressed, and as pert as she had been when we were both younger.

"I hope you don't mind my coming here," she smiled.

"Not at all. Sit down please." I dismissed the secretary and told her to close the door.

"It's nice to see you," Sarah said.

"You look smart."

"I'm not being a maid these days."

"How is Mr Peters?"

"All right. How is Mrs Pooter?"

"Little Posh is all right too," I replied. I wondered whether I should tell Sarah the truth. I was bored with Little Posh who had once seemed so lively and seductive. She had tried designing hats for women but had no talent it. She now spent her days sitting in our house, doing nothing much. As a result when I got home, she complained I was late and, then, had nothing much to say. A year after our marriage, I found myself in Chelsea and walked without thinking into the Russian Palace.

"Mr Perkupp," Madame Romanova said enthusiastically.

"My real name is Pooter."

Fifteen minutes later, I found myself in yet another gilded bedroom with Nina who said she was from Moscow but had never got nearer to that city than Moscow Road in Bayswater. I didn't linger long so Little Posh never found that I'd broken one of the Ten Commandments as Gosse's father would have put it. I got in the habit of breaking it twice a week. I almost did not know why.

"How did you find out where I was," I asked Sarah.

"I kept in touch with Mrs Pooter. "

"Oh, she never said."

We both became quiet. I'm not sure for how long. We both sat down.

"You seem miles away. Thinking romantic thoughts about Little Posh," she smiled.

"You see into my mind," I smiled.

What was on my mind had nothing to do with Little Posh, of course. Looking at Sarah, I was thinking back to our bed-tussles at *The Laurels*.

Sarah coughed. "You may think it odd, you may think it a cheek, but I've got a business proposition for you. I always had more brains than you thought," she said nicely.

"I never thought you were dumb."

"See what you think of this then," Sarah said. Peters had no spark, it seems. She had been trying to get him to agree to use their savings to set up a wine shop like no other. "Not French wine but wine from unusual countries." She went on to explain there were good vineyards in America, Australia, even the Levant. No shop in London sold them.

"Exotic wines from exotic places," I found myself saying.

"What do you think?"

"What do you want from me?"

"The money to do it right."

"So we don't see each other for years and then you turn up wanting cash."

She stood up to go. I stood up too.

We faced each other. For some moments, we said nothing. Then we started laughing. A few seconds later, I moved close to her – and kissed her.

"You're a married man," she objected, for a split second.

"You're a married woman." I countered. As she didn't move an inch back from me, I grinned and kissed her wildly.

"I didn't expect that," she smiled a few minutes later. We quickly agreed that we would go into business together.

"Are you coming to see me soon again," I asked.

"I'll show you the plans in detail tomorrow. But nicer to do it at a hotel. Your secretary keeps looking at us."

The next afternoon I took a suite at the Savoy Hotel. Sarah arrived on time. We kissed, cuddled and finally made love six years after we had first snuggled and not quite done it in my bed in *The Laurels*.

"Shall we have champagne," I said.

Sarah was always practical. "Let's see what exotic wines they have."

We ordered the wine list and, when we had studied it, we complained to the waiter who brought it, that nearly every bottle was French, Italian or German. Sarah told him she was shocked the Savoy did not have any Chateau Musar. "It is one of the oldest wines from the Levant. The crusaders drank barrels of it apparently. A top class hotel should be able to offer it."

"I will tell the manager," the waiter said meekly.

"The Savoy can be one of our first customers," Sarah said after the man closed the door behind him.

"Let's kiss to that," I said. "Tongue tricks, wasn't that what you used to say?"

"Good memory," she laughed but then stopped, stern. "Do you sleep with Mrs Pooter?"

I sighed.

"Don't lie, Lupin."

"Christmas and birthdays last year."

To my relief she giggled. "Same as me and Mr Peters. More a damp squib than a marriage."

"If we'd got married, do you think we'd be Christmas and birthdays too?"

"It's someone's birthday every day of the year, Lupin."

We went back to bed. Then we went to supper. Sarah gave a splendid performance as a worldly wise traveller who was so disappointed The Savoy Grill only served the most obvious wines. The *sommelier* was not used to being questioned in such detail, but rose to the occasion and offered us a fine port on the house.

A week later, after we had made love riotously at Claridges (one afternoon) and passionately at The Regency (very late), Sarah decided she would tell Peters he had to pack his bags, but she was kind and had arranged rooms for him with a rather motherly landlady. Eventually Peters and the landlady got married.

Little Posh did not prove so compliant, alas.

From then on, Sarah and I became what we had always been destined to be – best friends and faithful lovers. I only went to Madame Romanova's once and that was with Sarah. First of all, she was curious; second, she saw no reason why the Palace of Russian Beauties should not serve exotic wines ordered from Sarah's Spirits as we had decided to call our company.

"You are an interesting young woman," Madame Romanova said.

"I could have ended up here, you know," Sarah told her, "but Mr Pooter's mother was kind to me. She warned me not to fall in love with him till he was free."

"And what has happened to Mr Perkupp. He no longer needs beauty?"

I told Madame Romanova that he had closed the firm because he could no longer keep up with the world of modern investments. He had bought a house in the countryside and spent his days growing roses.

"The girls said he was not that passionate and often fell asleep," she said. "Many felt insulted. And when my girls feel unwanted, I double the price."

Sarah and I left the Palace hungry for each other.

Just after the end of the century, Perkupp's firm closed. Pa became depressed as if his whole life had been meaningless. We invited him and Ma for dinner at a restaurant that was one of our customers. We drank Chateau Musar and I asked Pa what he wanted to do.

"I suppose I'll have to do something to earn a living." It turned out that there was rather less money left for pensions than Perkupp had promised Pa and the other clerks.

"I have plenty of money, Pa," I said.

"I couldn't borrow from you."

"Then why don't you come to work," I was about to say 'for me', but I thought that would sound triumphant," at my office. Not as a clerk, of course. We need.."

"You don't need me Lupin," he insisted.

"He needs, he always has, needed you," Sarah intervened.

"You have been in the City a long time. Your experience will be valuable," I smiled.

So I found Pa a berth in my berth. He spent days reading the financial papers and, as a result, we sometimes recommended unlikely shares to our clients. Some were a disaster but a few did exceptionally well. Pa's worries about Communism made us a lot of money as we suggested selling Russian stocks short just before the 1905 revolution, which made the bottom fall out of the Moscow market.

The one problem I had still was Little Posh. She had taken to drinking far too much. I went home less and less and, when I did, she made scenes. She knew about Sarah. I went to see Daisy and asked if she could help.

"I wouldn't have bored you," Daisy, always the flirt, said.

"No," I smiled.

"And you love Sarah?"

"I always did. I was just too stupid to see it."

"You were young. We were all young."

"We're not so old now," I replied.

Daisy was kinder than I had imagined. She and Murray invited Little Posh to live with them.

After the fortune we'd made on the Russian stocks, Sarah and I took Ma and Pa to dinner at the Savoy. We had a soft spot for the hotel – for romantic reasons, and also because they ordered our Chateau Musar by the crate load.

We toasted or good fortune in vintage champagne – not the 3/6 stuff from Jackson Frères.

"This isn't just sentimental, Pa," I said. "You've earned us a lot of money and I think you should use your share to buy a house at the seaside for you and Ma. You've always liked Broadstairs."

Ma looked amazed. Pa started to dub his eyes. "Lupin, I hope I have been as kind a father as you have been a son."

"You have been, Pa. More than."

Across the table I held his hand. Ma started to cry too.

Sarah and I took them to Broadstairs a few days later and booked them into the Grand. Ma loved looking at houses especially as they could afford any one they wanted. They eventually settled on a detached place with turrets on the sea front.

"I can wake up and look at the sea," Ma smiled.

We helped them move in. Sarah organised two maids because Ma and Pa were getting older and would need more help.

They had five comfortable years in Broadstairs – and were looking forward to many more. Both seemed in good health for people of their age.

If writing this has taught me anything it is that you never know what life will bring. Ma liked to feed the seagulls and was sure they loved her. One gull didn't, however. The monstrous bird with a monstrous beak started pecking at her face. Ma collapsed. Her heart was weaker than anyone knew.

Her death hit me hard – and Pa harder. We couldn't leave him alone in Broadstairs and persuaded him to come and live with us.

Gowing died not long after. I did not tell Pa the truth about him.

"You know what I think would cheer us all up," Sarah said when we held each other in bed after we had made love. I still found her enticing, seductive, clever at loving.

"Surprise me."

Our first child was born nine months later. With Daisy's help I finally persuaded Little Posh to give me a divorce.

"Will you marry me," I asked Sarah a few days later as we were doing what never bored us.

"Better late than never," she grinned.

By the time we tied the knot, we had Charles and Emily was on the way.

Pa loved being a grandpa. It was while he was rocking our second daughter, Jemima, that, finally, he told me the truth about his bank robbing jail bird father.

"No wonder you wanted to be respectable," I said.

"I've always been frightened someone would find out I was the son of a criminal."

"I better tell you Cummings' secret," I smiled.

Having money does make it possible to do things. I had employed a private detective to learn the truth about Cummings. He had been in jail for embezzlement, but he had cleverly managed to hide his criminal profits by investing them abroad. He was often absent because he had money in France and he feared that if he transferred it through banks, he would give himself away.

Pa boomed with laughter and invited Cummings round the next evening.

"I know the truth about you," he said nicely.

Cummings turned beetroot.

"My own father was in jail too. He tried to rob a bank. Not very cleverly."

They became better friends than ever after the mutual confessions.

Pa turned 75 as the Great War started. He was getting frail and often dozed in an armchair after dinner. Our two maids made a great fuss of him. One night when we were alone, he suddenly said: "I tore those pages of the diary out myself, I'd been rude about you."

"I always wondered if you did, Pa."

"You've become quite smart," he smiled.

He petered out peacefully a few days later. I was at his bedside, holding his hand.

I took a large advertisement in the Ham and High which had been the local paper for *The Laurels*. It said:

Lupin Pooter, his wife Sarah and their children are sad to announce the death of their beloved Pa, Charles Pooter, author of the well-known Diary of a Nobody. Mr Charles Pooter was quite somebody, in fact, a clever man of finance and a fine writer.

We buried him with some ceremony. As we were toasting his memory, I hugged my three children and said: "I hope I'll be a good father to you as he was to me."

"Why shouldn't you be," Sarah said. "But I want one promise."

"What's that?"

"You'll never keep a diary."

Picture Credits

The original edition had some fine pen and ink illustration by Weedon Grossmith. These include the picture of The Laurels (p. 2), Mr Pooter painting the bath (p. 5), the author (p. 10), various pictures of Mr Pooter with his friends, Gowing and Cummings (p. 30 and p. 31), Daisy Mutlar (p. 44), the three friends (p. 66 and p. 97), perfect Perkupp (p. 70), Mr Padge (p. 84), Murray Posh (p. 132) and Hardfur Huttle (p. 136).

The cartoon of the life of the clerk is from *Punch* (p. 53).

The poster of Henry Irving as Dracula was included in Bram Stoker's 1906 memoir of the great actor.

The illustration of Samuel Pepys is from the frontispiece of his famous diary .

The cover of *Joe Miller's Joke Book* is from a 1943 edition.

The Russian beauties were snapped by Mrs Romanova herself.